Beasts in Their Wisdom
Stories by Eugene K. Garber

Snail's Pace Press, Inc.
Cambridge, New York

For Jan and her rousing troop of literary *bons vivants*: Amy, Barbara, Claudia, Joyce, Judy, Kazim, Lori, Peggy, Pete, Ron, Steve, and those yet to be drawn into the ambit of irresistible enticement.

Beasts in Their Wisdom
Stories by Eugene K. Garber

Snail's Pace Press, Inc.
Cambridge, New York

The Snail's Pace Press
Cambridge, New York
snail@poetic.com
Darby Penney, Publisher
Ken Denberg, Editor

The Snail's Pace Press is a member of The Council of Literary Magazines and Presses (CLMP).

This publication is made possible with public funds from the New York State Council on the Arts, a state agency.

ACKNOWLEDGMENTS
The following stories previously appeared in literary journals:
"The Goat," *Groundswell*, Volume 1, Number 1
"An Old Dance," *Kenyon Review*, New Series, Volume II, Number 1
"The Casita," *Black Warrior Review*, Volume IX, Number 1
"A Child of Fire" (as "The Island"), *Seattle Review*, Volume V, Numbers 1& 2
"The Uncle," *Kenyon Review*, Volume VIII, Number 2
"The Hunter," *Prism International*, Volume XIII, Number 2
"The Bird Watchers," *Michigan Quarterly Review*, Volume XIII, Number 1
"The Flight," *Paris Review*, Number 90
"The Oddment Man and the Apocalyptic Beasts," *TriQuarterly*, Number 61.

Front cover: *Feral Angels* (mixed media) by Lynn Hassan
Illustrations: Lynn Hassan
Back cover photograph: Anne Zilch
Cover design: Darby Penney

First edition January 2004

ISBN 0-9575273-5-X

CONTENTS

FAMILIES_____

THE GOAT

The aunt came to take care of her niece after her sister died. She hadn't even known her sister was sick, so word of the death came like a blow across her ear. "Get out!" she said to her man, Charlie.

"What the hell did I do?"

"You kept me tied up here while my sister was dying."

"I never heard of your sister."

"That's exactly it. You're not the kind of person anybody would ever mention a sister to."

Charlie threw his hands up in the air. "You crazy bitch. Frank said not to get mixed up with you."

"Get out."

Charlie scooped up his belongings and left. The aunt took a plane to Seattle, where her brother-in-law picked her up in a Peugeot station wagon.

The aunt despised her brother-in-law, but on the plane she tried to put that out of mind. She hadn't seen him in several years. Maybe time and death had changed him. Besides, it was her duty to console— not only the father but also the daughter, her niece, Melissa, whom she remembered vaguely as a wonderfully gay little girl. She would be twelve now. Nevertheless, the aunt hadn't been in the car with her brother-in-law for ten minutes before the antipathy welled up so bitter in her throat that she thought she would choke. He was exactly the same—his red hair brush cut, his eyes pale blue and inhuman, his carriage like that of a Marine colonel, his voice absolutely level and insistent. He was worse than Charlie. Charlie was merely ignorant and unthinking, but this man was inherently brutal. Even the way he held the steering wheel in his hand was an act of dominance. Well, so what? The aunt knew men. They didn't frighten her. But she couldn't stand the idea that he had been married to her sweet sister Andrea.

"Why didn't you let me know?" The aunt tried to keep anything accusatory out of her voice.

"That was the way she wanted it. She didn't even let her close friends know."

"I didn't think she had any close friends." The aunt kept her voice even, but she hoped it would be obvious that she was referring to the isolation of the house and to the endless trips her sister had to make with him, whether business or tennis.

"They were close enough. They would've come if she'd wanted them to. But she only wanted Melissa."

"Could Melissa do everything she needed?"

"Until the last few days. Then a nurse came in."

Already in her mind's eye the aunt could picture the desolate house, the rooms wandering along the ridge, everything a different level, the rocky inlet of the sound releasing fog like tainted breath, the bronze-barked madronas twisted as if by bone disease, the huge firs, the mushrooms, the ferns, the elephant cabbage, and always the dripping, the dripping.

"Melissa is very lonely," the man said.

For a moment the aunt said nothing, shocked anew by the way the man drained from every statement the slightest hint of natural sentiment, reducing everything to a low drone of insistence. Oh, how she would like to goad him until he bellowed passionately, but she kept her voice even. "You should've had another child." When he said nothing, she pressed him. "Well, why didn't you?"

"That was the way she wanted it."

"Or the way you wanted."

"No. The way she wanted it."

Melissa had grown, of course, and in her growing had come to resemble her mother more. She had the same dark blond hair and the high cheek bones and long patrician face that the aunt had envied so much as a girl—and as a woman, too. But the eyes, unfortunately, she got from her father—cold, metallic blue. "Give me a hug, honey." The aunt grabbed the child and held her close. She meant to establish an immediate rapport. The father left them alone to talk. Melissa cried a little, from which the aunt learned that when the face showed emotion, the eyes softened, but when they were dry again, the iciness returned. It was not something Melissa could control, of course.

"You were her nurse, Melissa. You will always remember that."

"Yes, but a real nurse had to come."

"Toward the last, sure, but no one could have expected you to do everything."

Melissa nodded, but remained silent. The aunt said, "Sometime, if you feel like it, I would like to hear a little of what she said since I couldn't be here."

"I wrote some of it down," said Melissa, her eyes hard and blue.

"Keep what you have written. It will be a treasure for you."

"Yes."

Meanwhile, Melissa took the aunt out to see the little shed and the corral. It was mid-morning, a Monday in late October. The father had gone to work. Melissa would not go back to school for a few days. Earlier, from the kitchen window, they had seen the yellow school bus pass way down below on the winding road, like a child's toy. The aunt remembered seeing, down at the foot of the drive, the little shed the father had built for Melissa to wait in. The aunt formed a vivid picture of the girl sitting there in her yellow slicker, the only splash of bright color amid all that gray green.

Tip, tick, tip, tick went the drops, though the fog had lifted from the inlet and patches of blue sky were visible through the firs. Why, wondered the aunt, did anybody live in this part of the country? They could send workers to get the wood and salmon, but not make anybody live here. Inside the corral were a little mare and a billy goat. Melissa opened the gate and led the way in. She carried a maple sapling branch thick with leaves for the goat and two apple halves for the horse. The mare was a sweet little animal, something between a pony and a quarter horse. She ate the apple delicately from the flat of Melissa's hand. But it was the goat that seized the aunt's attention. Perhaps she had never before seen a goat so close—the hooves cloven, just as in the stories, the horns thick and ridged, the penis and cullions trim and furry. And the eyes, the eyes. The irises, if they were irises, shone a beautiful gray. The strangely rectangular pupils were dark, of course, but at a certain slant revealed below the surface a milky blue. If cats in their half dozing closed the world to cuspid slits, then this animal saw the world as one huge bluish rectangle. He stripped the leaves from the sapling branch voraciously and ground them in his teeth with a curious circular motion. Oddly, he didn't smell. The horse did, but the goat didn't.

"What are their names?"

"Molly and Jewel. Jewel could jump the fence if he wanted to, but he's decided to stay with us." When the goat had finished the leaves, he pranced about for a moment, and then he ran forward and butted the horse in the flank, hard enough to make a resounding thump. The horse laid her ears back and turned to face the goat, but the goat went bounding away in a series of high angular leaps to show the horse that pursuit and retribution were not to be thought of.

Melissa took Molly to her stall in the shed and fed her hay and filled her water bucket. "The hay smells sweet," said the aunt. "What is it?"

"Mostly timothy and alfalfa."

The goat dashed into the shed and thrust his forefeet against the half door of Molly's stall with a great clatter. The horse looked up with apprehension. "Get down, Jewel," said Melissa, but did nothing to enforce her command. The aunt grabbed a horn and pulled the goat back. She wanted to make contact with the animal, domesticate it to her touch before it assumed too large an image in her mind. But the goat shook its head violently, and, if she hadn't let go of the horn immediately, would surely have twisted her wrist. "Well, he's a willful creature, isn't he?"

"I should've told you not to grab him by the horn."

"How do you control him?"

"You can whack him with a folded newspaper. He doesn't like the noise. But you don't really need to. He knows when to quiet down."

At that very moment, in fact, the goat stood almost pensively by his feed trough and waited for Melissa to fill it with pellets. The aunt touched the animal's neck. The dark gray coat of quite short hairs was smooth and sleek. "Do you have to curry him and comb him?"

"No. The horse, but not the goat."

From the shed they took a path that led a roundabout way through the woods back to the house. On the way, they passed what Melissa called "the jungle swing." A huge hemp rope almost three inches in diameter was tied to a stout fir limb above. The rope hung down some forty feet toward the floor of a deep ravine. "How does it work?" said the aunt.

"I'll show you. You pull the big rope to you with this guy." Melissa hauled in on a looping nylon line attached at one end to the big rope and at the other to the trunk of a small alder. When the big rope was within reach, she grabbed it, wound it once around her waist, and cinched it up.

Then, after reaching up above her head to get a good purchase on the hemp rope, she ran to the edge of the ravine and pushed off into the air. Away she swung out over the ravine for what seemed to the aunt long seconds before the small body reached the end of its moment and began to swing back. Slowly and then faster and then slowly again, Melissa came back, set her feet safely on the lip of the ravine, unwound herself as from the coil of a serpent, and presented herself smiling to her aunt. Her pretty dark blond hair was still swept back over her ears as if it kept beneath its shining surface a remnant of the wind created by the plunge.

The aunt took her niece's hand and pulled her away from the precipice. "What if you don't make it back and just keep going slower and slower like a run-down clock?"

"That's called letting the cat die. If you do that, somebody has to pull you back up with the guy."

"What if you're by yourself?"

"Then you have to pull yourself back up, but it's hard work."

They passed by a muddy pond. "My father was going to make a trout pond, but something keeps it muddy all the time. We don't know what."

Not far from the ridge they came to the tennis court. Rhododendrons grew just outside the fence. Inside, the neat green rectangles and white lines enclosed by the equally neat large terracotta rectangle seemed out of place amid the dramatic asymmetries of ravine, forest, and broken sky. "Does your father play here often?"

"Hardly ever. He and his partner and their coach play at the indoor club in town."

"Do you play?"

"A little. Most of my friends don't like it. Do you play?"

"No."

They followed the path along the top of the ridge back to the house. All around them were the twisted bronze trunks of the madronas. And down below was the road to town, twisting along the flank of the ridge. At the moment, the inlet was clear and sunlit, and the sky was blue. But off in the woods the aunt could hear the tick, tick, tip, tick of the recent fog.

That afternoon the father came home in a stylish sweat suit, navy blue with white stripes on the sleeves and pants. He carried his work suit in a plastic bag. He took a shower and came out into the kitchen with gray wool pants, a white shirt, and a red cardigan buttoned half way up. "Are you cold?" he asked the aunt. "We don't usually crank off the furnace until mid-November, but we can make an exception."

"I'm fine. How was tennis?"

"Fine. You want a scotch?"

"Sure."

When he had fixed the drinks and handed her hers, he sat down by the window. "What's for supper?" he asked with keen interest.

Already, thought the aunt, everything was domestic. The sister was entirely forgotten, another come to render the necessary services. It was the way they all were, never really weaned. "Hamburgers, cooked on the grill outside. Corn and potato salad. Pure Americana."

"Great." The father drank some scotch. "What did you do all day?"

The aunt smiled. That also was typical, the assumption of lassitude. Women spend several hours of each day luxuriating in their own grease, accumulating the soft subcutaneous tissue and the unctuous fluids that so pleased men. "We looked over the property, fed the animals, talked, that kind of thing."

"Did Melissa show you the other car and tell you where the keys are?"

"She mentioned it, but we didn't need to use it today. Tomorrow we'll take it in to the grocery."

"Take time one of these days to drive down the sound to Nusquam."

The aunt nodded. There was another assumption: she had all the time in the world. She said, "I don't think you really have to worry about Melissa. She's a strong girl. I'll stay until the end of next week. I have to get back to the shop." That about the shop was a lie. The owner didn't care when she came back. It was a pick-up job in any case.

The father spoke. It was as if he'd read her mind. "Is it a job you're really committed to?"

"They're getting close," Melissa called from the grill on the deck.

"O.K. I'll put the corn in." The aunt was glad for the interruption. It gave her time to think, but in the end she decided to tell the truth. "No, I don't care anything about the job. The merchandise is high quality. You don't mind selling it, but that's all."

"I wondered," said the father, "because Andrea said that freedom was your first consideration in all matters."

"Did she say that?"

"She said that all your life was a fight for freedom. She said you were a prisoner to the idea of freedom."

The aunt nodded. That had an authentic ring to it all right, because Andrea loved paradoxes.

Melissa came in with the grilled hamburgers, and they ate. After the supper things were done, the aunt lay on her bed in the guest room and flipped through some magazines her sister had subscribed to. She didn't want to talk to Melissa or the father any more that day. Later, she took off her clothes and put on her nightgown. But while she was naked, she stood in front of the full-length mirror attached to the inside of the closet door. She admired herself. But she was not a narcissist. In fact, she freely admitted, her body was not classically proportioned—the torso relatively short and the hips and buttocks too prominent for current tastes. But what she especially liked about her body were the muscles and the shading—the calves, thighs, and groin powerfully strung, features that showed particularly well in the slant light of the closet. It was a Celtic body, she believed, inherited from her mother, nee Murray. She felt a mild twinge of regret that she had gotten rid of Charlie in the anguished moment of learning of Andrea's death. He had shared her admiration of her body. But he was a stupid man. She would find a better one.

The aunt put on her nightgown, got under the covers, and turned off the light. She began to think of her sister Andrea, but to her surprise she did not feel sorrow. When she had first heard of her sister's death, it had had a terrible impact, but now it was more of a mystery, a problem. Not the bad luck of being stricken at age thirty-eight. No need to think of that. But the process of dying, the wrapping things up, the selection of what to say and do, the meaning of it. How could you fight clear of this last onslaught against your freedom?

Just before she went to sleep she thought she heard the horse neigh. It was not an intense or fearful neigh. Probably the goat had gotten prankish again. But what if a catamount had come down from the mountain? Penned in the corral, she couldn't run.

II

The next day, Melissa read to the aunt from the book she had kept during her mother's dying. The two of them were sitting on pilings at the end of a jetty just north of Nusquam. It was low tide, and the gulls were screaming and swarming over the mud flats. At the end of the jetty, just off the road, was the dead sister's yellow MG that they had driven down in, the top back. The sky above was blue and gray, the clouds so low and tattered that they had no delineation. Out in the sound rose a humpback island, its low forest releasing shreds of mist like the remnants of dozens of campfires.

"Not even this is virgin timber," Melissa read. "One day she went way over past the old tracks that ran to Seattle and bushwhacked into a marsh, and still she was stepping on little hummocks of feeder timber. She tried to remember the name of the machine the wildcat loggers used. Maybe it was a donkey. It was run on steam and made a terrible hooting and thumping noise."

The writing was in a small black loose-leaf binder, which Melissa did not choose to put in the aunt's hands. The aunt respected this, guessing that the entries were rough and that Melissa was not so much reading as reconstructing from notes and from memory. But what she didn't understand was why Melissa flipped back and forth in the book. This annoyed her. How could she tell anything about the progression of her sister's thought? Still, she didn't protest but let the child do things her own way.

"Then one day she went another way and found traces of an old skid road and went all the way over the first mountain and down again until there weren't even any fern anymore but only mushrooms and elephant cabbage and once a beautiful trillium. Until she came to a clearing full of fireweed and there was a little old red-bearded man. He was eating a wild crabapple and gave her one but it was so per...persimmonish? Is that right?"

"Yes."

"So persimmonish that it shriveled up her lips and she had to spit it out, which made the little old man laugh and show his teeth, which were all red and black from eating nothing but crabapples and berries. He was standing by a rusty old machine. 'You want me to fire her up?' he said, and she said no, but he piled the wood on and lit it. The machine steamed and hooted and thumped. The little old man laughed with his red and black teeth. And she ran away." Melissa closed the book. "I don't think that was something that really happened."

"No," said the aunt. "I guessed it wasn't. Didn't she say so?"

"No, she just told some things that were real and some that weren't and mixed them up together without saying which was which."

The aunt drove them in the little yellow car back up the winding road along the sound. The car was a joy, as she had known it would be from the moment she opened the garage and saw it sitting there, the brightest thing in sight. It was the only worthwhile thing she knew of that her brother-in-law had spent his money on. The sound of the little motor bounced gaily off the walls of rock and went careening down toward the sound, where the gulls variously glided, quarreled, and scavenged.

That afternoon, when the father drove up in his Peugeot station wagon and got out with his sweat suit on, the aunt said, "I need to get some exercise. Why don't you teach me how to play tennis?"

"Well..." The father hesitated.

"Come on. Melissa is watching the casserole, and I've got my shorts on." The aunt stood, arms akimbo in a patch of sunlight darting under the trees. Her breasts were big under the long-sleeved olive tee shirt, and her thigh muscles made a dimple above her knees. She wore tennis shoes without socks.

"All right," said the father. At the tennis court he stood at the net and threw a basket of balls to the aunt's forehand. "We'll just do forehands this afternoon," he said. She began to hit them back regularly. "You're a natural," he said. "I figured you would be."

"How?"

"You can usually tell people with athletic ability from their carriage and their body control."

"I never do anything athletic at home."

"Yes, you do. You can't help it. Like a cat that just loafs around the house. The natural athletic ability moves around inside no matter what you do."

The aunt thought about that. It must be true. Why else would her body be so firm and muscular? Nevertheless, the certainty of the man with the blue eyes and the red brush cut hair annoyed her. Nothing in his eye suggested admiration or even interest, but only calculation.

The next day the aunt and Melissa didn't drive out in the yellow car. They stayed around the house, walking in the woods nearby. For lunch they had some mushrooms that Melissa picked, porous things shaped like ears of corn. They were rubbery but flavorful. "These aren't magic mushrooms, are they, Melissa, that will make us see strange sights?"

"No." The girl smiled, softening the cold blue of her eyes. Her dark blond hair shone in the light of the window, and her long face remained elegantly refined even when she chewed.

A minute later the aunt smiled and said, "You fooled me, Melissa. They're working on me."

"What are they doing to you?"

"They're making me very forward."

"What do you mean?"

"They're making me say that although you're a rather formal young woman, I think I love you." Melissa looked down. "Don't be frightened, Melissa. I don't mean that I'm going to make love to you."

"I know," said Melissa quickly, but continued to look down.

"I've hurt your feelings, Melissa. I'm sorry. But you're the one that picked the mushrooms." The aunt chuckled. Then, when they stood up to clear the table, the aunt said, "Come here, Melissa." She held the child, who at first only submitted and then hugged her aunt back. "There. What kind of hug would you say that was?"

"A strong hug."

"Was it trustworthy?"

"Yes."

"Good. Actually, I would prefer not to love you, Melissa."

"Why not?"

"Because love robs one of freedom. But we have no choice." The aunt sighed dramatically and smiled. "The heart rules." It was necessary for the aunt to turn the matter off comically because she hadn't told the girl the whole truth, and she didn't like to conceal things from those she cared about. It was true that she didn't desire the girl physically. Nevertheless, she would like to open her up, force out the woman that was hiding behind the blue eyes. Why in this case she chafed so impatiently against time and natural processes she could not have said.

In the afternoon they went to the shed. Melissa took the animals their usual snacks. When Jewel had quieted down, they sat in the grass outside the corral and Melissa began to read, or reconstruct, from the black book, flipping again among the pages. The aunt didn't object. "She was remembering last winter, the winter of the catamount, when the snow line was so low that the top of the closest mountain was white. She feared that something was going to go wrong, so she walked around the property every day. It rained and rained, and when it wasn't raining, it dripped—tick tip, tick. The madronas on the ridge lost all their...supple?"

"Yes, suppleness."

"And groaned until she thought they would shatter in the wind. There wasn't even fog to soften the cold, because the rain and sleet knocked it down as soon as it tried to rise off the sound. The pond was like brown glue, but something lived in it and swam just below the surface—a sucker or a sculpin. How could a fish get in the pond? From the eggs in bird droppings, my father said. You couldn't make the jungle swing work. The thick air killed it. So every time you had to let the cat die and pull yourself back up by the guy."

"Did your mother swing on the jungle swing?"

"Oh, yes, she liked it the best of all of us." The aunt was amazed. Melissa went on. "Down in the shed, where Molly stayed most of the time, you couldn't smell the timothy or the goat pellets. The thick air killed it. You couldn't quiet Jewel down. He twisted his head and threatened to butt you. So the animals knew. She told my father. At midnight he fired his shotgun against the mountainside and he left the light on in the shed all night. But the catamount came to get Molly. My mother heard its growl droning in her sleep, but she couldn't wake up. Maybe she was afraid and was a coward." Melissa flipped the pages of the black book anxiously. The aunt waited.

"She could see it, the cougar with the reddish brown coat winter-thick and dusted with snow. Molly neighed and reared in her stall, but it was Jewel that drove the cat off. He rammed it in the ribs with his horns. The cat screamed and slashed the air, but the goat ran at it again. The cat fled back to the mountain. The goat and the horse won, she said, because they had more of the world in their eyes. The cat had narrowed everything down to a mean slit."

The aunt nodded. "Could you see the tracks of the cat the next day?"

"No, it rained all night, she said. What you could see was that Jewel had dominance over Molly, and still does. She might lay her ears back and turn to kick him, but in the end he gets his way."

The dark gray coat and the big eyes of the goat came into the aunt's mind. But she was wise enough not to try to puzzle out the meaning of the story of the cat, or of the little old red-bearded man either, for that matter. She would listen to the rest and then it would come clear. "How much have you read me?"

"Not quite half."

"Are you going to read it all to me?"

"If you want me to, but some of it is about you and your mother."

"Yes, I want you to, but not any more right now."

"All right. "

The aunt slipped away from Melissa and went to the jungle swing. The floor of the ravine was dark. Only here and there a narrow ray of sunlight struck through the canopy of trees above and lighted up a yellow alder leaf as though it were on fire. She hauled in the thick rope. It was coarse and prickly to the touch. Nevertheless she wound it about her waist and cinched it as she had seen Melissa do. It was tight and did not slip when she tested her weight against it. She must push off hard, she knew, to produce a swing powerful enough to bring her back. She did, her legs strong against the face of the ravine. But she didn't kick out evenly. Consequently, as she went down, she began to spin slowly so that not only did the floor of the ravine rush up at her with its little dots of fire, but the trees made a dizzy rotation. It was only luck that she came back facing the lip of the ravine, but it wasn't just luck that she loosened the rope about her waist at the proper moment so that it didn't tip her back. Actually, she was never physically afraid. If she hadn't gotten back and had been forced to let the cat die, she knew that she was strong enough to haul herself back up by the guy. Nor would that have mattered much. Her aim was not to perform a feat. It was to experience what her sister Andrea had experienced. Nevertheless, she was glad that she made it back, for she was sick, not in her stomach but in her head.

She had known that she wouldn't like the swing, but she hadn't predicted the absolute revulsion she felt. What had happened to cause Andrea to crave the diseased titillation of the swing? It was all right for a child, the derring-do, the little death, but not for a grown woman. And these dying fantasies of cougar and leprechaun, for God's sake, they were part of the same complex. In effect, Andrea had killed herself. Well, that was too strong, but she had let the cancer in. She had slipped into some kind of unreality that had climaxed in a private and fantastical dying. The aunt went away from the ravine almost in tears. The physical loss of her sister had been a blow, but this evidence of the destruction of her psyche was more than she could bear. What had caused it? Maybe it was the blue eyes. Man, child, and goat—not a natural pair of eyes on the place, not even Molly's, too huge and brown.

The aunt arrived at the ridge. In the weak sunlight from the motley sky over the inlet the madronas seemed softer, more comfortably gnarled. But she was still bitterly angry, so the reconciliation of madronas to wind was only an irritant. She put them behind her and went on to the house, where presently the father came. He seemed disappointed to find her in jeans. "Aren't we going to continue with the tennis?"

"I have to chop things for the omelets."

"I can do it," said Melissa.

So the aunt went back and put on the shorts and the tight jersey. Under her brassiere was a thick rouge ring where the rope had chafed. The sight of it made her angry, and she was glad to cover it up. On the court the father threw balls to her backhand. Again, she quickly got the feel of it, hitting with both hands on the leather grip. But after a few minutes, she was embarrassed by her absorption, even though the man could not possibly have guessed her turmoil of only a few minutes ago. "You're supposed to be teaching me," she said. "You aren't saying anything."

The father, shaking his head with genuine amazement, said, "Natural top-spin on the backhand."

"What's that?"

"I don't want to tell you anything. I don't want you to think about anything. Just keep doing what you're doing." He backed up with his racket to the end of the court. "I'll hit you some. You'll miss the first few because they come different. Don't worry about it."

She hit two or three on the wood and then she saw that she had to move faster. She began to hit them back, long arching shots to the baseline, and he kept the ball in play for her, a very nice rhythm. But after a while this began to seem self-indulgent to her. She lost the feel of it and stopped. "I have to go in and help Melissa."

Again, before going to bed that night, the aunt stood naked in front of the closet mirror. How dark she was, darker than when she'd come. There was a dark fluid that lived below the skin, she understood, put there by inheritance, called forth by the sun. So even the faint intermittent sun of the mudflats and the tennis court had darkened her. It was almost frightening to have a darkness within oneself that leaped up to the sun like that, but it was also a strength. Nothing could blanch her. Could death blanch her? Only if she lost her dark fluids.

So she was the darkest of all, her mother's child, a Celt. Never mind that before she died her mother became a repressive bitch. That was because of the church and her father. Who was her father, anyway? She could barely remember him, a haggard and worthless man named Olney, who had succumbed to an early and cowardly death. Thank God she had inherited nothing of him. But Andrea had. She was lighter and finer, and now she was dead. And the terrible thing was that Melissa had inherited not only a portion of her mother's lightness but her father's also. Poor child. What the aunt wanted to do was this: strip all the clothes from the girl and lie with her, fold her in her arms, turn her this way and that, touch her in every place until she had bequeathed darkness to her. There was nothing perverse or fanciful in this, for the aunt knew that she had in her skin a subtle olive fluid that in warm contact with the girl she would exude.

The aunt sighed. But perhaps it was fanciful, after all, for there would be no way to break through Melissa's inhibitions and misinterpretations. The aunt put on her nightgown and went to bed. She felt unctuous and potent and utterly wasted.

The next morning was fine, still and sunny, the tip tick tip tick of earlier rains and mists driven deeper into the woods. Shortly before noon, after she'd fed the animals, Melissa got the black book and said, "Let's go down to the tennis court. The concrete gets nice and warm."

The aunt was amazed at the low but persistent warmth that emanated from the green surface.

"This is about my father."

"Good."

"She said the first time she met my father, she thought he was just a boy. He was like one of those big bronze-colored puppies whose paws are still too big. But he wanted to be very dignified. He spoke with a low voice. They met in the office, where you couldn't say anything personal because that was the company policy. So she had to quit and move to another office. He took her to the tennis club and the yacht club and down to the famous wharf restaurants in Seattle." Melissa turned the pages of the black book. The aunt looked up at the sky and said, "Melissa, I don't think we'll see another day like this. I'm going to get some sun." She took her clothes off, tossed them aside, and lay on her back on the warm green concrete.

"My mother said to my father, 'You always take me where there are people and man-made things.' He laughed and asked her what she wanted. She said she was a girl from the Midwest, and the rocks and the forests amazed her. That's what she wanted. So they came up here on a picnic, walking the old overgrown tracks before there was even a road. They spread their blanket out on the ridge by the madronas and looked out at the sound. And that was the first time she relented. She did it on purpose where she wanted to live."

This disgusted the aunt. Bad enough to use one's body to calculate one's future home, but was it necessary to tell the girl? Did death require the revelation of all the troughs of one's life? The aunt must unwittingly have made a face because Melissa said, "You want me to go on?"

"Yes. I want to hear everything. But why don't you take your clothes off and get some sun?"

"What if somebody comes and sees us?"

"They will either admire our innocent naturalness, or they will look at us with concupiscence, in which case their eyes will be plucked out by hawks." The aunt laughed. "I'm not kidding, Melissa. This is a country of moral absolutes."

Melissa took off her clothes and sat with her knees up. The aunt raised her head and looked down the length of her body at the girl, whose breasts were just barely beginning to swell. But at that moment, the aunt's own breasts were also very modest. She laid her head back down, looked up at the blue sun-suffused sky, and laughed. "Where do a woman's breasts go when she lies on her back?"

Melissa smiled. "I don't know."

"I think they don't trust us. They're always afraid we're getting ready for a man. So they try to scuttle away down into the rib cage. But they can't. They're too plump. They get caught, like fat little garden thieves in a picket fence." The aunt laughed. "Melissa, what do you think of all this crazy talk of mine?"

"I like it."

"Do you? Why on earth do you?"

"Because it keeps everything from being so dark and serious."

"Good. Read on."

"Well, they were married and living happily in a waterfront apartment downtown. And while the house was being built out here, I was being built in town. We came at the same time."

The aunt lifted herself up on her elbows and looked at Melissa, who sat with her knees up and her legs crossed daintily at the ankles. Behind, in shadow, were the vulvae, ruddy and enclosed in a light tufting, as of winter rye. "And you, Melissa, were a thing of beauty, whereas the house . . ."

"The house is beautiful," said Melissa with an insistence that surprised the aunt.

"Well, yes, I guess you would have to say it's beautiful. Your mother would've made sure of that. But I don't trust it. It doesn't seem to know where it wants to be. It wanders this way and that, up and down."

"That's because of the stones. It has to follow the stones of the ridge. That was the whole idea. Just like our bodies have to follow the concrete here on the tennis court."

"Not mine. Simply by flexing the muscles of my buttocks, I could press a comfy little dent here in your father's playground. But I won't. I don't want you to know yet that I have supernatural powers." The aunt laughed and lay back down. "Read on."

"This part came after the nurse was here. My mother said my father wanted another child, but she wouldn't give it to him because she could see what it was going to be. She could see it fighting against his rib cage and plunging down between his legs to try to get into her and be born. It was a little boy as white as snow. She couldn't stand the idea of that icy little being inside her. He would have blue diamond eyes that would cut her to pieces. She said there was already too much ice blue in me and this other would kill her." Melissa paused. "This was when the nurse went to my father and said that my mother was out of her head and saying things that I ought not to hear, much less write down. But my father told her to let me hear anything I wanted to and write it down."

"So what else did you hear?"

"She just said the same thing over and over. That the little snow boy was still beating inside my father, but she couldn't bear him. She cried, but she couldn't bear him, she said, because his ice would tear her to pieces." Melissa's voice faltered.

The aunt got up and went over to sit by the girl. She put her arm on her shoulder. "You don't have any ice in you, Melissa, except a little accidental illusion of frost in the eyes. So don't worry about that."

"But I'm not as warm as you are. I can feel it in your arm."

"Ha!" said the aunt, taking her arm away and waddling heavily toward her clothes. "Nobody is as hot as I am. Didn't I tell you that I have supernatural powers. I'm an earth goddess with a molten core. Beware."

When the father got home, the aunt was ready in her shorts, her tight Jersey, and her sockless shoes. She had washed none of them and they were beginning to have a distinct odor that she found pungent and pleasant. But he in his glamorous blue sweat suit smelled like nothing. "Let's hit them back and forth again today," she said.

"That's the idea," he said, smiling.

They hit for a while. The aunt watched the little green ball right into the racket. She pretended that she was hypnotized. She couldn't take her eyes off the ball. The eyes were mad with desire for the ball and sent frantic messages to her legs—oh please get me to the ball! It was fun. She laughed.

The father shook his head. "I've never seen such a natural. Can I be your agent?"

The aunt had forgotten all about the father. The ball didn't come from him. It was something she willed—imperfectly perhaps, because sometimes it didn't come exactly where she wanted it. But it was she who willed it. So she wasn't happy to be reminded of the father. "No," she said, "you cannot be my agent."

He shook his head sadly and hit her another ball. She began to hit them harder, outside the court. "Hey," he said, "you're supposed to hit them inside the lines."

"No, I'm not. I'm supposed to hit them anywhere I want to, and it's your job to get them back inside the lines."

He laughed. "All right."

She knocked them as hard as she could. Go away, she would say to the ball, fastening it with her eyes. Don't come back. But it was amazing how often it came back. The father would lunge and leap and hit them out of the air. This went on for some time and then they stopped. They were both breathing hard. The father said, "That's fun, but it won't go over big at the tennis club."

"No, I suppose not."

"Well," said the father as they walked toward the house, "What's for supper?"

"We didn't fix anything. We thought you could take us out."

"You bet I will," said the father, immediately pleased with the prospect. "We'll go down to Oyster Cove."

That night when she lay down in bed, the aunt thought of the snow boy, as she knew she would. She didn't even have to begin to drift off to sleep before the images of him grew strange and potent. This comes, she said to herself wryly, of pretending to have supernatural powers. He was there in the cage of the father's ribs prowling like a cat, blue-eyed and cold and yet foul with imprisonment. How could a being so icy stink? But he did. She saw him beat against the crosspieces of the corral. Molly's nostrils flared and she laid her ears back. And the goat Jewel came prancing and curious, tossing his horns with a sudden verve, as if to say, What is this wonderful rank creature? Shall I nuzzle it and welcome it, or shall I destroy it with my horns? The aunt was half asleep now. She chuckled wickedly. The goat thought that his strength was all in his continence, like the runner she had dated in high school, who thought that his semen was like Samson's hair until she drained it from him and he discovered that he could still walk and talk and, yes, even run. And that was enough of him. It was the snow boy she last saw, his sharp blue eyes peering angrily out at her from the bars of night.

Melissa went back to school. The aunt walked with her down to the little shed to catch the school bus. It was raining, just as the aunt had first pictured it, and they both wore yellow slickers. The one the aunt wore had belonged to her sister. Perhaps that was why the faces of the children in the bus window looked so astonished. To have a schoolmate who had lost her mother would be a rare and tragic thing. But for the schoolmate to discover a substitute mother was even stranger.

When the aunt got back to the house, the father was still there, dressed and ready for work, but he didn't leave immediately. He stayed to have a cup of coffee with the aunt, who said, "It's about time for me to go."

"Will you really?"

"Yes, of course."

"What about your tennis career?" The father smiled. The aunt didn't bother to answer that. "Then, what about Melissa?"

"Melissa's all right."

"Why do you want to go back? You don't have a man."

"How do you know?"

"If you had a man, he would've called you."

The aunt smiled and sipped some coffee. "Let's say I'm between men right now."

"All right. Then why do you want to go back?"

"Well, let's see. In my apartment I have a closet with some clothes and a dresser and some books and records and tapes and so on. More or less like a normal human being."

The father shrugged irritably. "You're not telling me why you want to leave us. We can send for all that."

The aunt noted for herself that she didn't hate the father, though she still had a residual desire to prick him to some impropriety. "You've got it backwards. I'm not leaving here. I'm going back where I came from."

"But for no reason."

The aunt peered comically into the father's cold blue eyes. "Is there some reason you want me to stay?"

"Ah!" The father again showed impatience. "Melissa wants you to stay. I want you to stay. For all I know, the goat wants you to stay."

"Oh, the goat. He's horny for me, but I shall not yield. Yes, and Melissa and I are chummy. But I didn't realize about you."

"Yes. I, too, have succumbed."

"To what particular facet of myself, may I ask?"

The father smiled beneath his crisp blue eyes, "I don't know you well enough to tell you."

"You can tell me anything. I've told you as much."

"Yes."

"Then go on. Tell me."

"Well, I would say the thighs, principally. Wonderful thighs."

"The thighs, principally. I see. And not the breasts? Because, you know, I had them nicely tricked out in the Jersey."

"Well, yes. The breasts, too." The father stopped smiling. "It might sound silly, but I'm serious. I want you to stay."

All this while, of course, the father's voice had droned in the aunt's ear not only with its silly images but with its authority and insistence, and still she hadn't struck out at him. Why, she wondered. "Look," she said, "what you want is a younger woman—to start a new family with."

"You're younger, and still fertile, I imagine."

"Yes, but I'm already entangled in your old family. You want your children to be their own cousins? The church declares it incestuous to marry your wife's sister."

"We're not talking about the church here."

"Nevertheless, what you want is a real breeder. You can be the paterfamilias. The woman can be the mother and Melissa can be the little aunt and the ridge will swarm with children. Oh, happy day."

"What do you have against children?"

The aunt saw the snow boy urgent behind his eyes. "Nothing," she said, "nothing at all, except the bearing of them."

"What have you got against the bearing of them?"

"Well, they occupy your body, you see, and you have no choice. And then when they want to come out, you also have no choice. They open you up and rip you apart."

The blue eyes contracted. The aunt understood why. The man had already had one woman who wouldn't bear him a son. How well did he understand, she wondered. When he looked in the mirror could he see the snow boy beating behind the blue ice of his eyes? At this moment, he didn't know what to say. He drank the rest of his coffee and looked intently at the aunt. The aunt said, "Think of another."

"I don't want to think of another. I've seen you and I'm thinking of you." He got up and went off to work.

It was drizzling and all around the house the trees were in a frenzy of dripping. Tip tick, tip tick everywhere, as if deliberately to aggravate the aunt's agitation. She put on a slicker and went out to the corral with a halved apple and a maple sapling. How incredibly bright the yellow rubber of the slicker was. Where did all this light come from under those gray skies? She shook her head. It was not light, of course. It was just the unnatural dilation of her eyes. In this awful dun world everybody's eyes—man, woman, and beast—swelled with hunger for light and imagined all sorts of bright images—red beards and fires and fireweed. The goat snatched the branch from the aunt's hand and tossed it viciously as though it were something he had to kill before he ate. Molly came over daintily, placing her feet carefully in the soft soil, and took the apple from the aunt's flat palm. How gentle the little horse's eyes were, but bruised nevertheless by the darkness of the land. When the goat had stripped away the leaves and ground them in his teeth, he came prancing up to the aunt, lifting his head gaily and shining his big eyes at her. The goat was insane. There was no principle of gravity in him. "You are insane, Jewel," said the aunt. The goat stopped dead in his tracks and tilted his head and then shook it as though a strange sound were burring in his ear. The aunt laughed aloud, the sound bouncing from the trees even in that heavy air. The goat squared around at her and lowered his head. "Oh, my God," she said, "I suppose you're going to butt me to death for insulting you." But the goat never as much as made a feint. Instead, he tossed his head up airily and trotted off to menace Molly for a moment and then he disappeared behind the shed.

In the afternoon the aunt walked down to the road to meet Melissa. When the bus pulled up, she watched carefully to see how the others treated her. There were perhaps a half dozen to be dropped farther out along the sound. All stopped talking and waved good-bye, all rather subdued and respectful. Melissa said good-bye to them and stepped gracefully off the bus. As they walked back up the hill, the aunt said, "Your schoolmates know that you have gone beyond them, not just because of your personal qualities, but also because you have suffered and are deeper."

They walked on for a while and then Melissa said, "No, it's not that."

"What is it, then?"

"It's you.

"Me!"

Melissa smiled happily at the aunt's astonishment. "Yes. All the strange things you've told me and the supernatural powers you've touched me with."

"You don't mean to tell me that you've told your school friends all that."

"No. Of course not. But that's what makes me different."

The aunt shook her head wonderingly, though the gesture was not entirely ingenuous. "Well, what about the things your mother told you? Surely they're as strange as anything I've told you."

Melissa turned and looked out at the aunt from beneath the hood of her slicker. The face, encased in bright yellow, and especially the cold blue eyes, were even more severe and patrician than usual. And alas, thought the aunt, somewhat deluded in their new sense of power. "Maybe," said the girl, her voice pitifully brave with the veneer of wisdom, "they were as strange or even stranger. But they weren't as strong. They didn't mean as much to me."

The aunt nodded and then said, "Nevertheless, you still haven't finished reading me all of them. Have you?"

"No." Melissa seemed reluctant.

"It's the part about my mother and me, isn't it?"

"Yes."

The aunt laughed. "Oh, my. Is it so bad that you don't want to read it?"

"No, I'll read it."

They sat in the living room in the bay window overlooking the sound. "You take the window seat," said Melissa.

"Yes," said the aunt, curling luxuriously among the lush pillows. "It doesn't sound like I can take this standing up. I'll lie here and look out into the gray mist, where the awful images of my mother and me will materialize."

Tip tick. Tip tick. The water fell from the eaves of the house onto runways of shiny aggregate. Melissa began. "My mother said that her mother was a cave woman, a wild druid that worshipped stones and mistletoe and circles of laurel. Until a man named Olney came from across the sea and dragged her out of the cave and down to the city and civilized her. She tried to learn manners, and she did learn the surface of them, but she couldn't pack them down into her soul. There was a dark cave there, but it wouldn't admit Olney's white civilization. It was full of smoke and clubs and animal pictures and beat Olney's civilization back. This is what killed him. He was left on the outside in the winter to freeze." Melissa flipped forward through the pages and then back again.

"The worse thing that could have happened to the mother was for the father to die. It turned all the civilization she had learned against her and made her fierce with guilt so that she was determined to bring her two daughters up as ladies. The older one was fine. She had a long face and knew how to act. But the younger one was a throwback with a wide face and dark skin. She didn't know how to act. So the mother beat her. But all that did was make her skin even darker and . . ." (Melissa paused, to get the next phrase exactly right) ". . .dilated the dark portals even wider."

"Yes, go on."

"My mother said she watched and wept, but it wasn't because she felt sorry for you. She wept for herself. She longed for the stripes and the wisdom of the bruises. But it was too late for her to defy her mother because your defiance had drawn all the mother's anger to you. So she wanted to lie with you and extract from your body some of the darkness and the bruises. She said she thought if she didn't get some of the darkness and hurt she would die." Melissa looked quizzically at the aunt with her cold blue eyes, which were bruised already by wisdom.

"Did we ever lie together? That's what you want to know, isn't it?" She was angry. Who would have thought it was such a boon to be beaten? So privileged, in fact, that you were compelled to share it, to be with every cold and blue-eyed creature that expressed admiration for the darkness of your skin, your thighs. The horrible logic of this was that to save them from death she must lie with Melissa and the father and the goat and even, the snow boy. This extravagance pleased her and made her eyes flashing hot. "Go on," she commanded.

"That's all there is." Melissa closed the black book and held it out almost apologetically. "Would you like to see it? I might've left something out."

The aunt started to reach for it, but then shook her head. "No, I'm sure you've given me everything, the essence of everything." But what she was thinking was this. What if the book contained only a scrabble of notes in no apparent order? Then the child's reconstruction would be too uncanny. The aunt would be put at a disadvantage.

Melissa set the book down but continued to look at the aunt out of her cold blue eyes that were glistening with a childish but deep desire. The aunt said, "Take your clothes off, Melissa, and I will take mine off and we will lie together." And then as they were putting aside their clothes she said, "We should have done this on the tennis court with the trees and the blue sky to witness our innocence because houses tend to give everything an illicit flavor. But this will do. We have a big window."

Melissa lay on her back with her eyes closed, but she wasn't stiff. The aunt shook her black hair down over the child's face and kissed her copiously. How surprisingly warm were the child's eyelids and lips. The aunt lay beside her and folded her in her arms, turning her gently so that all of the child's body was exposed to her hot flesh. The aunt was aroused, but that was a distant sensation, secondary to the extraordinary seepage of darkness. She could feel the olive fluid, the hot exudate pouring from her into the child. And the amazing thing was that it didn't diminish her but augmented her. She herself was darker, fuller. She opened the child's thighs and pressed against her and lay heavily on her, breast to breast. She turned her and pressed down on the thin buttocks. However, she did not open the labia with her fingers or force her tongue into the child's mouth. And at the last, she sat apart almost chastely and stroked every part of the child once more as though she were anointing her with oil. Her fluids subsided and she began to feel a slight chill. The child breathed deeply and opened her blue eyes to the aunt. The eyes darkened as the afternoon dimmed. The child sat up and took the aunt's hand and kissed it hesitantly.

When the sound of the father's car came, however, Melissa started up and gathered her clothes. "Sit down, Melissa," said the aunt, but the girl was frightened, poised to fly. "Sit down!" The aunt flashed her eyes at the girl as if in anger and amazement. "Will you turn us into a couple of naughty school girls?"

"No. But I'm afraid."

"Sit down, please."

Melissa sat down but with her clothes clutched to her breast and her back to the door. The father came into the doorway, started, and then peered into the dim room. "What are you doing? My God! What in the hell are you doing?"

"Be quiet," said the aunt. "Everything depends on your being quiet." There came a tense silence then, but she knew already that she had won. The man was not full of prudery and repression. There was more to him than that.

"I'm waiting," he said, but his face was aflame. Even in the dim light the aunt could see that, or sense it.

"Be quiet," she said. "If you fume, you will never understand anything." She let the silence well up again until the tip tick tip tick was quite distinct. Then she said, "Melissa has been telling me all the things her mother said when she was dying. You should hear them some time. You're not absent."

"I'm not in question at the moment."

"Oh, yes you are. You were a red-bearded leprechaun with berry-blackened teeth and a horrible pounding machine."

"Talk sense, for God's sake. I come home and find you naked with my daughter and you tell me I'm a leprechaun!"

"Be quiet. When we had heard all that her mother said, we held each other close. Melissa was full of sorrow and fear of death. You understand what I'm saying. Tell me that you understand and have cleared your mind of filthy schoolboy imaginings."

The father sighed and ran his hand through his hair. "Understand it? No, I don't understand it, but I don't believe you are perverted."

"Thank you."

"Oh, for God's sake! Put your clothes on. And then you'll have to pack and get out of here."

"No, I will not leave."

"You will not leave my house if I tell you to?" The father laughed sardonically. "We'll see about that."

Melissa's face had lighted up gloriously when the aunt said she would not leave. She turned suddenly to her father. "We will never lie together again,

Daddy. We only had to do it this once."

The aunt laid a hand on Melissa's. "We will do whatever we need to do, Melissa. Your father understands that."

"How can I understand, for God's sake?"

The aunt walked directly to the father and looked in his eyes. She knew she would triumph. Still, she pitied him. For the snow boy was beating behind his cold blue eyes, oh how wildly. The man had no hope of overcoming his inner necessities. She said, "You asked me to stay. I accept."

The father looked at her, taking his time, sizing her up pitilessly, looking frankly at her body there in the dim light.

"Let her stay," said Melissa.

The aunt waited for the man to speak, and while she waited, she felt a twinge of fear, for she could see in her mind's eye the man's huge body, brutal in its whiteness except where the hair sprang out like fireweed. She could hear the awful machine of his sex. And then would come the insemination and the disfigurement and the wretched pain. But the baby she would have no trouble with. No matter how cold and blanched he was born, she would fill him with such dark refulgence that he would outbrazen the sun.

"Come with me," said the father, "Just as you are. We have to settle how things will be."

"I will wait here," said Melissa.

Then, as she followed the man toward his widower's bedroom, she thought of the goat. Later, she knew, she would weep for her dead sister and for the unction of dark love that she, the younger, locked in her own childhood suffering, had not shared. But at this moment, the sister was a negative principle. She could not be saved. Melissa could, the snow boy could, and even the man, despite the diamond hardness of his eyes. Ah, and the goat. A mate must be found for the goat, or in his vaunting madness, in the wildness of his shallow eyes, he would bring the house down. The aunt smiled as she entered the dark bedroom. Glory to the goat.

AN OLD DANCE

 The sun requires blood. Our dancers know how to signify that, stooping, hanging their arms down together like huge lolling tongues. We are, all four of us, enthralled by the lurid set bathed in red, the deep pounding of drums and the dancers' high-stepping pantomime of angry hunger. Behind the scrim is the shape of the great pyramid with the god-house atop. A priest stands there, his obsidian knife raised on high. On the backdrop is painted a huge stylized heart, stubbier than a chicken heart, with twin volutes sprouting up, the aorta. It looks a bit like a space capsule plunging earthward. Our younger son Lane tells us that it ought to be pointed skyward. He has read the gruesome accounts of human hearts swiftly cut out and held, still beating, up to the sun. So there ought to be an upward motion, he says. It is fortunate that these pantomimes of blood sacrifice are extravagant and melodramatic. For if they were vivid, they might disturb Lane deeply, despite his mother's initiatory rites, just as his reading in Meso-American mythology disturbed him earlier. He is still too tender for this world. It is a question of certain endowments, emotional and physiological, involving empathy and the introjection of the feelings of all kinds of creatures. Lane's mother has said that it is like living with an emotional hemophiliac, an apt image, for it has often seemed that a deep bruise to his feelings would be fatal. This is the story of Lane's initiation in Mexico. His initiator was his mother. All the ancient rites call for the father to initiate the son, but I could not have done it. Lane's older brother, Michael, Mike, could have done it if it had been absolutely necessary, though they are only two years apart, fifteen and thirteen. Here is the difference in a nutshell. Just a few minutes ago we saw "The Ball Game" danced with a big plastic globe half the size of a weather balloon and only just heavier than air so that it bounced about among the dancers in an elegant lento paradoxically mixing images of inexorable momentum and weightlessness. On the one side of us Mike went through a passionate thermo-muscular dream of participation, unconsciously moving hips and elbows in imitation of the dancers. On the other side of us Lane whispered the possible significances: the ball was a human head buffeted by the contrary winds of fate but destined ultimately to pass through the hoop of immortality; or, the ball was the sun that went up and down, designating those to be sacri-ficed; or, the ball was the cosmos, the hoop the cosmos' own eternal round. And so on. And here is an image of Lane's mother. Some days ago at the charreada, the rodeo, when the young man bit the tail of the Brahma that had fallen into a wise placidity to avoid further lassoing, she laughed lustily and called, "Nip the loafer!" So she was the one who said of Lane, "He can't go through life like this. We can't go on protecting him."

"What are you going to do?"

"I'm going to show him things, show him everything."

"You'll kill him."

"Better his blood on my hands, who bore him, than for the world to kill him as soon as he steps out of our house."

At the Boxeo

We sat in the twenty-third row. On the white brightly lit square down in front of us there were to be five events, three prelims and two features. The finale would pit "El Tigre de Jalisco" against "Ishmael Toboac," the mad Jew of Buenos Aires. This was the first of the initiatory trials which Lane's mother designed for him. We did not at that moment know precisely how many there would be (a Herculean even dozen?) or toward what pinnacle of suffering we were ascending. While Mike strained forward in his seat, slugging it out with the boxers, Lane provided a gloss based on his extensive reading of Mexican mythology. For instance, the fights were under the auspices of the ancient god Tezcatlipoca, Lord of the Smoking Mirror. Of the smoke there could be no doubt, thick sickening stuff rising from cigarettes and Cuban cigars, hanging in the air like the viscid white gas that magicians pour from milk bottles.(Nothing so delicate as the scrim that partially conceals the priest with his obsidian knife.) The mirror image was less obvious. How, precisely, were we to see ourselves reflected in the two then fighting—a peppery Mexican with a thin mustache and a glistening black who had not kept his guard up and was bleeding from the left eye? Lane and I were the misfortunate Negro and Mike and his mother were the excoriating Mexican? No, because suddenly the black, who had seemed pinned against the ropes, came flashing forth, all glistening like the knife, and cut the Mexican down. The crowd roared. When he could be heard again, Lane tried to explain that the ring (curious misnomer, or is it?) was a four-cornered mandala encircled by the spectators. The fighters, paradoxically, an emblem of unity, revolved at the hub, the center of centers, which made the ring, like all mandalas, a quincunx. Precocity—nothing can be clearer—is a curse. Lane's mother hissed at him, "Stop talking and watch. You might learn something about the manly art of self-defense." So we sat silently through the rest of the bouts breathing the foul air, listening to the crowd howl, watching the boxers, whose leaden gloves prevented what might otherwise have been clean kills. El Tigre and Ishmael, incidentally, neither in great shape, fought to a standstill and fell into each other's arms, having only occasionally aroused themselves to a slow pantomime of trading blows. "One of your Aztec priests ought to finish them off," I said to Lane, but he was, in obedience to his mother, deep in suffering, his hands clenched, his face set, and his eyes narrowed but, bravely, not shut. I feared those images he was storing. (My wife and I had a friend who, after seeing that eye-slicing scene in *An Andalusian Dog*, had to go to a shrink and later a hypnotist to get the image removed from his inner eye, and still he lives in constant fear of its return.) "Remember Marvin," I said to her.

"Atta boy!" she shouted to El Tigre, whose fist was making its way slowly toward the thorax of the Jew. That night Lane had a nightmare. We heard him shouting out in his sleep. "Stop! No, stop!" We hurried toward his bed in the adjoining hotel room. When we got there Mike was still sleeping, albeit restlessly, and Lane was just struggling up from the abyss of fear, whimpering piteously. My wife shook Lane's shoulders. "Wake up, Lane." She had snapped on the ceiling light and flooded the midnight room with blank glare. Lane blinked his eyes. "What's the matter, son?" she said. Lane looked at his mother's face. Some moments passed before her presence displaced the images of his dream. Then he said, "He was after me."

"Who was after you?" my wife said, at which moment Mike suddenly sat up in his bed. The question had struck through his sleep and alerted him that information of interest was about to be revealed. He looked at us brightly, angrily. "El Tigre," said Lane, "with his claws." So the dream figure was of much greater ferocity than the slogging boxer of some hours before.

"No he wasn't," said my wife. "You have been here in the room with Mike all the time, and nobody else has been here. Isn't that right, Mike?" Mike fairly glowered as he nodded his head—Mike the empiricist. All things material glow in his eye with luminous solidity. Not for him the second images, afterimages, fleeting auras of dreamers. "See?" said Lane's mother, who possessed the same bird-bright eyes as her Mike. I should have shouted, "Be quiet, ignorant inquisitors! Blind in your inner eye, you know nothing of dreams and dreamers." But I was silent while Lane, aware of the futility of arguing, merely nodded assent. "Then go back to sleep," his mother said. "And put your mind on not dreaming. Mike is here with you. And we're next door." Mike nodded peremptorily, as though to say that his role as guardian of Lane's sleep was too piddling to warrant full acknowledgement. If on the other hand, there had been a real tiger at the gate, let it be said for Mike that he would have gladly thrown against it all the strength of his young body.

"OK," said Lane. My wife snapped off the light and we went back to our room, where I said, "This is a dangerous game you're playing." She looked at me sharply for a moment. "Game?"

"Tactic then—of suddenly filling Lane full of fearless macho."

She shook her head slowly. "I'm not that stupid. I know it will not be suddenly, if ever."

"Why not just let him be whatever it is he's going to be."

"What? Cringing, hypersensitive? You would be satisfied with that?"

"I would learn to love him whatever he was."

"Yes, of course. So would I. But why give up without trying? Why not work for something better?" I had no ready answer for that. My wife lay back down in her bed, turned her back to me, and soon fell asleep.

The dancers have assumed a different posture. No longer do they hang their arms down in front like blood-lapping tongues. On the contrary, they are standing erect. They have thrown their heads back and are addressing themselves to the gods of the red sky. Into their mouths they have inserted long feathered things like Halloween serpents that uncurl and whistle when you blow in them. These scrolling songs, sayings, chants, whatever, Lane tells us, are very similar to those seen in the codices. So, everything in this extravagant performance retains an element of authenticity. That's good to know, but the truth of the matter is that we are too caught up with the dancers to pay much attention to Lane's gloss. What's fun is to try to figure out the nature of each of these plumed orisons. For instance, one tall male is suavely waving a spray of peacock blue, obviously the language of court flattery, the Aztec equivalent of The *Book of Common Prayer*. One of the women is making an undulant motion with a golden spray of softly sweeping marabou feathers, an aspirant to celestial courtesanship. I plan to try to identify each of the eight dancers and later test my characterizations against my wife's, which will be just a hair too cynical. But now Lane whispers, "I like the green one best." He's a nice choice all right, a maize man, tall and straight, with a topknot of yellow tassel. Not only does he aim his spume at the sun, but in his fervor leaps up into the air. Perhaps even my wife will be pleased with Lane's choice. In the meantime, Mike is saying, "Mine is the red one." Of course. He's a brilliant crimson. Byronic, out of patience with the gods, he shakes his red plume at them ferociously, like a fist. And what do the gods do, these ungentle Aztec super-beings who live in sun, volcano, and thunder? Why, at least for the moment, they are much like our modern gods—entirely otiose.

At the Corrida

This was the most predictable and the most lachrymose of poor Lane's trials of manhood. Even so, there were some omissions from the scenario which would have made the event even darker. For instance, none of the picador's horses were gored. None of the banderillos were thrown, though that would have been luckless and untoward indeed. No young boys were impaled on the bulls' horns. One did jump over the wall with a cape, but half-heartedly, and was quickly thrust by the matador's assistants back up into the stands. "What was he trying to do?" said Lane.

"He was like those boys we saw in the park yesterday with capes, only he wanted to try it out on the real thing," said my wife. "Pretty brave, huh?" Lane nodded. He tried to please his mother by taking, like Mike, a great interest in the particulars of the corrida. But when the second bull had fallen to his knees vomiting blood, and there were four more to come, Lane could not fasten his mind to the events in the ring. Instead, he began his mythical meanderings.

Mumble them softly to me, I wanted to say to him, so that your mother doesn't overhear. And for a while it happened that way. He whispered to me about the acrobatics of the great bull-leapers of ancient Knossis, about the labyrinth in the center of which bull and man were one. But Labys was the name of the Ax God and he didn't see how that fit. Needless to say, I could not illuminate the matter for him, though, God knows, if a large displacement of time be allowed, there was before us ample butchery and blood to image a great deal of axing. In fact, the third bull was at that very moment being dragged away, and the fastidious rakers of the sand had not yet appeared to cover the blood. From the labyrinth of Knossis it was an easy step to the omphalos, which we had already seen, you remember, at the charreada and at the boxeo. And because the matador wore a cap with black bull's ears and his hair in a pigtail, it was easy to see that, appearances of conflict notwithstanding, bull and man were actually one, just as boxers were one with each other and ropers were one with calves and ponies. Well, I thought to myself, Lane's is a complex case. Either all this comes out over and over again because of the intolerable pressure his mother puts on him, or he is a hopeless obsessive, or he is a true mystic, which in the contemporary world is defined as insanity. Which should I hope for? Meanwhile his mother inevitably overheard some wayward remark about how the initial allegorical procession, led by the somber premonitory figure of the black horseman, was tied in with the ring's cosmic divisions—inner and out circles, sol y sombra. And she came down on him like the Mexican eagle on the hapless serpent. "Lane, for God's sake look at what's really out there, instead of at that childish myth stuff in your own head."

Later that night I made my wife a witty discourse on the metaphorical nature of all perception. "I admire the single-minded way you are handling Lane," I said. "I really do. But you can push your empirical line too far, you know, and undermine your own position—I mean insisting that everything simply is what it is. For instance, as you know, there are no colors in the universe, only light waves of certain lengths, which the optic nerves choose to represent as colors. And there are no caresses, no kisses, dear—only the repulsion of electromagnetic fields. So a person may make out of a bloody sandpit a number of things." To give credit where credit is due, my wife tried to take that seriously. She even went so far as to say that she bet some ancient philosopher had said that the best thing to do was to assume that what we saw was what was really out there. I told her that I didn't know of such a person, though Mike might grow up and say something like that. But she wasn't listening to me because she had gotten the giggles. "Kisses ... caresses ... electromagnetic fields," she repeated in a high whinnying voice, and then collapsed on our bed under the insupportable burden of mirth. So I was merely playing the pedant to her wholesome fleshy grasp of life. But the fact remained that Lane was genuinely suffering. Maybe it was true that the bullring was exactly a bullring and the matador exactly a brave killer and the dead bull a dead bull, but if Lane wasn't allowed to mythologize it, he got sick. So when the fifth bull fell dead, Lane got up and went down to the low concrete wall at the edge of the stands. He leaned over and vomited a yellow stinking mess onto the sand below. Good, I thought. He's made of it a toilet bowl, a piss pot, Mambrino's helmet revealed for what it is if myth is to be denied. And like all spiritual vomiters, he experienced a relief much more profound than can be explained by the ejection of indigestive elements. He looked back up at us with a smile that perhaps he intended to be sheepish, but that was really, at least momentarily, beatific. I said, "Lane and I will skip the sixth bull. We'll explore the nether regions of the ring. Maybe we can discover the place where they saw the animals up and dispense them to the poor." Neither my wife nor Mike acknowledged our departure. So that night when my wife had recovered from the near hysterics that my philosophizing had plunged her into, I said, "All right, laugh. But let me ask you one serious question. Are you keeping a careful eye on exactly how far he is from the edge?"

"No," she said flatly.

"Well, that's interesting," I said. "You just plan to keep pushing him until he drops over?"

"No, but if necessary until just before he drops over, in which case I'll catch him."

"My God. What monumental presumption. What if you don't see him start to fall? What if you're not nearby when he starts to topple?"

"Where would he be?" My wife seemed genuinely surprised by my question.

"Off, dear, in some pre-Columbian Aztec temple where the priests of Tezcatlipochtli, or whatever they call him, hunger for more blood sacrifices." I kept my tone serious, but she didn't answer me in kind.

"Phooey! I'll still reach out and catch him."

I shook my head skeptically. "I hope for your sake, as well as for his, that your mother intuition works out. Because if it doesn't, there will . . ."

"Be quiet," she said. "I know it."

After the acrobatics of The Ball Game, the lurid ceremonies of The Sacrifice, and the extraordinary synesthesia of Feathered Song, we examine our programs to see what's coming up. First, a ten minute intermission, which here in Mexico will be more like twenty, and then three more big numbers: The Clash of Flowers, The Plumed Serpent, and Coatlicue. Meanwhile we stretch and blink in the light that has gone up in the theatre. We seem to each other suddenly pale, watery-eyed, and vulnerable, as though the light has caught us out in a moment of private self-communing that ought to have remained hidden in the dark. Even the tough ones, my wife and Mike, appear momentarily weak, but they quickly stir themselves and hurry off to the lobby to see what's doing there. Left alone, Lane and I do not talk. Our silence is comfortable. We are both thinking that this, our last big event in Mexico, is really his. It is almost as though the choreographer had designed these dances precisely as a tribute to

Lane's successful passage through the severe trials of his mother's making. That may make it sound as though the issue were never in doubt, as though there were not moments when our presence here now would have seemed unlikely indeed. Even so, we both feel strongly that the dance is Lane's. And I for one am glad that the sacrifice at the pyramid came early in the performance and is done. So now, though I haven't read the descriptive blurbs about the dances coming up, I somehow feel both relaxed and titillated, a mood which is not disturbed when Mike comes back saying, "American guy in the lobby says the finale is almost too much to take." I am not disturbed, either, by my wife's sharp glance. She suspects that Lane and I have had soft and emasculating communications, a suspicion I will relieve her of later. But in the meanwhile, I am not disturbed by the perverse reversal of roles my wife's distrustful glance implies.

The lights dim and presently the curtain rises on The Clash of Flowers. "Blossoming War," Lane whispers to me, "is how they ought to have translated it." I see his point. The dancers who thrust and dart at each other are not just flowers, though they wear pale leotards embroidered gorgeously with luxuriant sprays of color. And there is not exactly a clash between them. In fact, it becomes clear that the dancers are also the bees and the humming birds and the butterflies that transfer the pollen. And as they stretch and leap, not quite vertically, they are also slant rain and shafts of sunlight. Toward the end they gather in and fan out to show the blossoming that results from the war. War, blossom—curious, but the dancers show that the paradox is true, leaning out from a sunburst center in petaled splendor.

At the Mercado Libertad

We entered from the plaza through a narrow corridor of flower stalls, fresh and fragrant after the swarming heat of the wide Calzada Independencia. But these pleasures were short-lived, for presently we passed into the dried flower section, which made Lane sneeze. A moment later we encountered a branching of ways—leather goods down one aisle, straw down another, and vegetables in a distant offing. "Which fatal fork here, oh trusty leader?" I said to my wife, who immediately whisked aside a hanging blanket of Indian zigzags to reveal a stairway. "Up!" Up was the eating section, a long series of once white-tiled stalls, behind which women and men prepared the famous chicken and corn soups of Mexico, the famous tacos of varied filling, the pigs' feet, the ribs, the huge crisp chunks of pig's skin, the messes of brains and kidneys, the shrimps and fishes, the pickled vegetables, and so on. And at the stalls, sitting hunched over plates, were the mid-afternoon eaters, spooning up soups, gnawing flesh from bone, crunching skins and crustaceans, rolling up tacos like fat cigars and engorging them in two bites. A grindery, a human mill for reducing objects of nature to the homogenous pulp of alimentation. And all around the place rose the heat, noise, and odor of mass ingestion. Did our leader whisk us through these unpleasant precincts? No, slowly, looking carefully left and right in order to take in the varied offerings of each stall, she proceeded deliberately, nay lovingly, like a connoisseur. And we behind, perforce, at equal pace. I noticed that not even her natural son Mike savored these refections. And Lane began to discolor. Fortunately we reached the end of the stalls before his stomach turned as it had at the corrida.

We passed among trinket stands and then entered—not an alley or a cul-de-sac exactly but a sort of close or mews, a congeries of tiny stalls selling herbs and other curatives. "Are you going to get us a joint as a consolation for that trip through the gastric inferno?" I asked our leader. That got a giggle from Mike, but it was perfunctory because we were all immediately fascinated by the wares—tangles of rank-looking weeds (emetics, no doubt, strong enough to unbind a mule), delicate sprays of dry lacey flowers (aphrodisiacs?), ugly black worts that looked as though they had been blasted by a hundred early winters, and much else. Our group broke apart as each of us found different centers of interest. Turning a corner, I bumped into my wife buying a little packet of black powders, "Sal Negra, Contra Malos Vecinos." I chuckled and passed on, browsing aimlessly until I happened on Lane standing agape in front of a stand which featured the hanging pelts and bones of small animals, also snake skins, strings of snail shells, and other zoological remnants. But it wasn't these that had so dramatically seized Lane's attention. It was the vendor, an old crone whose head seemed to hang there among the animal parts as within the wicket of an entry into the underworld. And what's more, so wrinkled was she, so withered her mouth and forehead, so warted and moled all over, so straggly with hair on chin and head that for an instant I thought she was hanging upside down, the famous sibyl in the bottle. But when she spoke I saw that her mouth was after all below her nose. "¿Qué quieres, niño?" She spoke in a high insistent quaver, but Lane said nothing. I nudged him. "She asked you what you want."

"I know that," he shot back petulantly, so I waited for him to say something to her. But he said nothing, just stood there looking at her, not looking at the interesting wares, but obsessively staring into the old woman's face. I grew embarrassed and blurted out, "Medicina contra una mala madrastra." Medicine against an evil stepmother. Well, I didn't have to dig very deep in my unconscious to discover where that came from. Fortunately Lane didn't know the word. (I hadn't known until that moment that I knew it.) "What's a madrastra?"

"Hell, I don't know. Something I read in one of the other stands. You weren't saying anything." He didn't say anything to that either. The old woman's mouth began to work obscenely, like an agitated anus. At length she said, "Muy raro, muy caro." Very rare, very expensive.

"Vamos a ver," I said. We'll see. She took down a little jar from a high shelf and set it on her tiny counter. I looked with amazement at the hand that set it there. So did Lane, I'm sure. The hand was not gnarled, knobbed, or warted. The nails were not cracked or necrotic. In fact, the hand was hardly wrinkled. I peered sharply at the woman in the wicket to see if the ancient countenance was really a mask. If it was it had been put on by a make-up man too clever for me. Meanwhile the anomalous hand was turning the jar so that we could read the label: "Malas Madrastas." So maybe I had actually seen the word displayed on something in a previous stand. I picked the jar up and inspected it closely, like a connoisseur. I perceived that a certain gamesmanship was necessary with this hag. I handed the jar to Lane. "Eyeball it carefully, son." Then I addressed myself to the hag. "Me parece heces del buho." I may have said that purely out of orneriness, but the fact is that the stuff did look like owl pellets, and I decided to make the pellets feces. But I could never have predicted the response I got. The crone threw back that withered rotten-apple head of hers and screeched like a moon-haunted owl—a screech so raucous and inhuman that it unnerved me. Lane widened his eyes, set down the jar, and would have backed off, but I was right behind him, standing my ground. I had to. "¿Cuanto cuesta?" I said, noting uncomfortably the thinness of my voice compared to the old woman's rich ululation.

"Una dosis cuesta veinte pesos."

"¡Ay, caramba!" I exclaimed, striking my forehead as in a seizure of penurious grief. "Muy caro." Well, everybody had told us that you ought to get anything in the market for half the initial asking price. But did I really expect the hag to come down? No, I did not. She puckered her anus mouth and said, "Vale mas, senor. Vale mas." It's worth more.

"Bueno," I said. "¿Es suficiente, una dosis?"

"Sí, sí. Mire, señor." She opened the jar with great care and sifted a tiny pellet out into the palm of her hand. Then with her free index finger she ground the gray substance into a fine powder, like graphite. "Miren, señores." She lifted the stuff ceremoniously, like a priest raising a chalice—up over Lane's head until it was very close to my nose. Then suddenly she leaned forward and blew sharply. Out of her hand rose a puff of gray smoke that flew over my shoulder. Did I say the mouth looked like an anus? The breath seconded the image. Or was it the odor of the puff of gray dust? I didn't have time to unravel this, because I heard a coughing and a disgusted poohing in my ear. I turned to find my wife beside me, her face bearing evidence of the hag's ashy ministrations. I couldn't keep from laughing. And once having started, I thought I had as well be hung for a goat as a sheep, so I let rip a series of raucous guffaws that bent me over against Lane and rattled my ribs. The crone joined in and treated us to another of her unearthly ululations. When I was sufficiently recovered to receive communication, my wife said, "Why don't you pay up and let's be on our way." First I had to settle accounts with the crone, who was holding out her gray-smudged hand. I fished up a twenty peso bill and laid it in her hand, tapping the paper significantly. "Mire," I said. "El famoso templo de

Quetzalcoatl y Tlaloc."

As we passed through the last of the herb stands on our way to the stairs, Mike, having formed up with us at this point, my wife said, "How long do I have?"

"According to the hag," I said, "not long. Any minute now you will start shriveling up and melting into the floor like the Wicked Witch of the West." But Lane wasn't smiling. I feared he was feeling guilty, thinking that we had perpetrated on his mother some aggressive act. "How about it, Lane?" I said lightly.

"She wasn't really a hag," he said. "She was an aspect off Tezcatlipoca, smoking mirror."

Down we went.

Even before I saw anything, I smelled the odor of flesh and blood rising up the stairwell. "Wife," I whispered, "I think we have seen enough of the great Libertad." But she continued to lead us down without comment. Perhaps if we had come early in the morning we would have seen attractive displays of chops, roasts, rolled skirts and the like. At least we would not have seen the absolute dregs—hearts, livers, brains, sheets of tripe, and organs I couldn't even identify. From long strings of hooks hung hogs' heads and feet and a few scrawny yellow-gray chickens. Elsewhere, on beds of bloody ice, large fish were beginning to make odorous announcement of their not so recent deaths. As we passed one stall, the butcher ladled briny water up from a rough tun and doused his festooning of hog's heads, which then dripped prettily from their pale lashes, pert ears, and gently smiling mouths. Noting—or to be more charitable, misin-terpreting Lane's gaping dismay, the butcher said, "¿Queres un puercito, niño?" With his fingers he widened the smile of a dead pig. Lane sidled away. But my wife approached. "¿Qué se puede hacer con una cabeza de puerco?" What can be made with a hog's head? The butcher rattled off something and then kissed the tips of his fingers, those very fingers which had formed the inviting smile on the hog's face. My wife went on playing the game, inspecting the heads closely, and Mike egged her on. "Get the one with the spotted ears, Mom."

"¿Qual, señora? ¿Qual?" The butcher was anxious to take one down and wrap it for her, become the first butcher of the Mercado Libertad to sell a hog's head to a gringa. "Para usted, señora, un precio especial." That was the last of the exchange I heard, because out of the corner of my eye I saw that Lane was at the end of his tether. A wave of pity rolled over me. Nightmares, vomitings, what would he have to suffer next? Fainting. How did I guess? I had something of the same feelings myself—that burred quality of all sound, the tendency of the whole spectacle of carnage to wheel as though one's spine were affixed to an axle of perpetual suffering. So I grabbed his arm and hustled him toward a splash of daylight I spied in the distance. The prospect of escape braced him. He walked most of the way under his own power. But before we reached the open air, he went limp, so I had to pick him up and carry him through the final hive of blood and flies. The patch of daylight I had spotted was a small interior patio surrounded by stalls of straw goods. I laid Lane on the stone floor. Several women approached clucking. But presently his breath came more regularly, his eyes fluttered hopefully, and he said, "I'm all right."

By the time his mother and brother had found us, he was standing, albeit weakly, drinking a Coke I had found nearby. "Lane and I are ready to be liberated from the Libertad," I said.

The dance of The Plumed Serpent is a disappointment. The costumes are gorgeous—scintillant green leotards, headdress of purple feathers, diaphanously winged arms. The dancers lock themselves together to form the long slithering image of the great god Quetzalcoatl. But the dance is inert—something to do with the god's profound benignity, which does not lend itself to drama. My attention begins to wander. I have an image of my father holding a forked stick like a witching wand, but he is not witching. He is stalking something that is running on the ground before him, a snake. I follow close behind him until finally he plunges his stick down like a little pitchfork and pins the snake's tail. "Watch!" he says. The snake struggles for a moment and then suddenly is on his way again. "Look," says my father. In the fork of his stick is two inches of the snake's tail. "It was a glass snake." He hands me the section of tail, broken off precisely along a seam of scales. And it does feel like glass— smooth, dry, and brittle. "How does he do it?" I ask. "I don't know," my father says. I try to hand him back the tail. "Don't you want it?" he says. "No," I say and drop it into the grass. My father says, "A coyote will chew off a paw to get out of a trap." Even when the temptresses of Quetzalcoatl come out in their whorish black pelerine-like garb, the dance will not come alive. (They are agents of Tezcatlipoca, I know this time without Lane having to tell me.) So my mind wanders again, this time to an episode in the childhood of one of my sons. I cannot remember which. He is sitting beside a tiny fence of white wickets that surrounds my wife's flower garden. Inside the wickets a little grass snake has been sunning. It is summer. The babbling of my baby boy has awakened the snake and set his little red tongue to flickering in and out. The two stare at each other a long time. Perhaps a primordial trust is rebuilding, which will erase the effects of the fall. But then my son reaches out a fat meddlesome hand. The irrepressible urge to possess is upon him. And away darts the little snake toward cover but he does not make it. The blade of a spade comes plunging down and cuts the snake's head off as clean as a guillotine. The executioner? My wife of course. The baby—I still do not remember which—sets up a piteous howling. "Bad snake," says my wife. "Bad snake!" But the baby, horrified by death or, more likely, peeved by deprivation, will not see the snake as evil. He continues to whimper and sob, and even crawls forward to retrieve the severed body, but my wife snatches him up, hugs him, and tries to console him. I cannot sympathize with her. I say, "What do you expect, killing a perfectly harmless garden snake?"

"Goddam you! I know it was perfectly harmless, but do you want him to get in the habit of ogling and petting every snake he sees? What if the next one is a rattler?" And curiously, perversely I think, the child stops crying and looks at me reproachfully as though it has suddenly understood that its mother is its protector and I am a dangerous sentimentalist. I turn away from them both. I will not accept the idea that to protect ourselves from a few evil things we must kill much that is innocent. Which son was it? I still cannot remember. Lane, maimed by the image of phallic destruction, or Mike, strengthened by his mother's unswerving tough-mindedness? How approximate are our histories. Unsortable even in cases as dramatically different as those of Mike and Lane. Now the snake dancers are climbing one upon the other, making a pyramid. The music is rising triumphantly. A resurrection is taking place, or a translation to the skies, but I haven't been paying attention and therefore don't know what's going on.

At Teotihuacan, City of the Gods

The question was whether to start with the Pyramid of the Moon and end with the Temple of Quetzalcoatl and Tlaloc or vice versa. We decided on the latter. Actually I was suffering a mild case of Moctezuma's revenge, and so the first sight of the vast expanse of the ruined city tended to depress me. But the Temple of Quetzalcoatl and Tlaloc was very moving because, finally, the disparity between Quetzalcoatl's benevolence and his representation as a curve-toothed serpent resolved itself for me. While Mike scooted around saying wow and looking from every conceivable angle, Lane and I studied the faces of the plumed serpent and the rain god. My wife walked the course set out for the visitor, slowly, giving the temple its due, but pretending no reverence. Anyway, as I said, the benevolence of the serpent came clear to me, although I cannot say exactly how, something in the deepness of the hollow eyes, something in the intricate scrolling of the ears—though all around loured gray stone, bare hills, and dry dusty plains inhospitable to man. No wonder Tlaloc seemed strained, popped-eyed. What will, even divine, could wrench from those desiccated skies water necessary for maize? So I found myself in a state of mildly mournful peace. But how precisely was Lane taking it, I wondered. He had come through the boxeo, the corrida, as well as the witch and carnage of the Libertad, but in what condition, having suffered nightmares, nausea, and dizziness? Was he weaker or stronger? At the moment he shared with me the sense of repose afforded by the shadow of the grinning serpent. I felt that strongly. But like the serpent heads themselves, braced with iron rods, his balance was precarious. Some final test of equilibrium was to come, the last rigor of his mother's tutelage. From the Temple of Quetzalcoatl and Tlaloc we went to a recent excavation revealing bathing stalls and some badly faded frescoes among which Lane thought he spied the Teotihuacano emblem of cosmic paradox, the flaming freshet, Burning Water. When we emerged from this underground place, we were met by a flautist. He was making a slow high glissando on a little clay pipe that was molded in the shape of a man. So the stops, as it were, represented perhaps a multiplicity of navels—or maybe the cruel perforations of the priest's obsidian knife, although the little face just under the mouthpiece was complacent, almost smiling. The flautist was a willowy young man not much older than Mike. He wore the inevitable huaraches on his feet. His pants were rolled up to the knee and were tied at the waist by a piece of rope. He wore a shirt the sleeves of which seemed to have been brutally hacked off with a dull knife. He had a little knapsack slung over his shoulder. He was a mestizo, his hair black, his nose sharp, his eyes narrow, his forehead broad, and his cheekbones flat. As I came up the steps from the excavation, I saw him silhouetted against the gray-bright sky, his fingers arched delicately over his pipe like a spider's legs. It was an image I knew I was destined to remember. We tipped the attendant who had guided us through the excavation, and he pointed us toward the ball court. The flautist followed us. "How do you like the music?" my wife said. Mike said, "I don't like it. It's fruity."

"Well, get used to it," my wife said. "The guide book says these tooters hang on like leeches. There's no shaking them."

"I like the music," Lane said.

Mike didn't pay any attention to that. "What does he want?"

"He wants to sell us a pipe," my wife said. "About forty pesos, as I recall."

"Then let's buy Lane a pipe and get rid of this guy."

I looked sharply at Mike, but I knew I wouldn't find any malice— unthinking cruelty maybe, but never malice. Give credit where credit is due. Meanwhile, the flautist was tooting a gay little scherzo that would've had us all marching in step if it hadn't been for the stony ground which broke the rhythm of our walking. "It won't work," said my wife. "If one member of a group breaks down and buys, then he hangs on until everybody does. We'd have to buy four."

"To heck with it, then," said Mike. "Let him follow us around. I'll bet he won't climb to the top of the pyramids." Lane lifted his eyes to the Pyramid of the Sun. "You mean you're supposed to climb that?" Actually, his question was already answered by the presence up there of a half dozen early-bird tourists. We could see them milling around against the gray sky. At the ball court Mike decided to run, "Just to get the feel of it," he said. So while we sat at the top of the stone stand, he dashed around down inside the court.

The flautist made proper music—a nervous, sometimes almost shrieking screed of presumably athletic sounds, but I myself found that the fluting had a decidedly hysterical edge to it, which reminded me that Lane had mentioned something about the ball being a human head. My wife, however, was at this moment reading aloud from the guidebook. "In this cosmic game, the ball, presumably the sun, which the players had to keep aloft lest it descend into eternal night, was made of hard rubber and probably embellished with carvings and golden paintings." She read on about the noble captains of the players, the probability of a hoop, the extant representations of players in elaborate collars and greaves. Meanwhile I watched our son Mike make swift runs along the sides, dash across the ends, feint, and pivot as though he'd been playing basketball down there in the rocks and dust of Teotihuacan ever since it was founded some 17 centuries ago. Something about his absolute grace in that confined space gave me goose bumps. (The music also added to the effect, the flautist inspired by Mike to great flights of trilling and shrilling.) I admired Mike, but my admiration contained an element of horror. There would always be, I was thinking, a class of noble warriors (Eagles, Jaguars were they here?) for whom war was as natural and necessary as breathing. And what could the peaceable weaklings of the world, like Lane and me, do to keep them from destroying us? Make up games, like the ball game—keep 'em running. That was the only hope. "Hey, let's give him a hand," I said. "Come on, Lane!" So we clapped and whistled and yee-hooed. "Who's winning?" my wife hollered. Mike drove under for a lay-up, then came running up the stone seats shaking a fist in the air triumphantly. The flautist produced a reasonable imitation of a tantara of victory, but I noticed that everything came out of that pipe in a minor key. Mike stood in front of us, arms akimbo, breathing only a little faster than usual. "That freak still following us around? Let's see if we can lose him on the pyramids." So we trudged off down the Avenue of the Dead, the Pyramid of the Moon directly ahead, the Pyramid of the Sun off to the right. It was toward the latter that Mike turned us when we drew abreast of its grand frontal steps. "Hey, wait a minute," I said, "don't you want to do the tallest one last?"

"No," said my wife. "The book says the visual effect is wrong. Also the Moon is steeper and ought to come after you've gotten the hang of it on the Sun." At the foot of the steps I looked up and shook my head. "How many steps does the book say it has?"

"It doesn't say," my wife said. "Just start climbing and counting and you'll know when you get to the top."

"Nope," I said.

"Aww!" said Mikes disgusted. "You're not going to climb it?"

"Nope. Moctezuma is raging in my stomach. I'll try again when we get to the Moon." I turned to Lane. "You going to keep your old sick Daddy company?" Actually I was not feeling that bad, but I thought I would give Lane an out. He suffered mild acrophobia. However, to my surprise he said, "No, I'm going up. You can sit over there in the shade." He pointed to a stand of three low scraggly trees—I don't know what, stunted peppers perhaps. So, he had seen through my ploy and was rejecting it. He wanted to brave it out, both pyramids, the whole thing. In my heart love and respect surged up—tempered, though, by worry. What if something happened and I wasn't up there to do anything about it? "Well, then . . ." I began. Lane shook his head, almost pleadingly, I thought. "Rest under the trees." He wanted to do this alone with the two fierce ones. "OK." My anxiety subsided. There would be no crisis on the Pyramid of the Sun. Something in its slope, gentler than that of the Moon, reassured me—something also in the timing, the arch of the day, which had not yet reached its crest. So, as they mounted the steps, I headed toward the meager grove. The flautist followed me. When I reached the trees I looked back and saw that the three of them had already reached the break that ran around the middle of the pyramid like a tightly cinched band. Mike led, his mother and brother keeping equal pace behind. I sat down in the shade and leaned against the trunk of the largest tree. I gave the flautist a ten-peso coin and told him to play me something soft. "Tocame algo muy suave," I said. I don't know if that was right, but he took my meaning and began to play a marvelously plaintive melody. I shut my eyes. The first thing I noticed was that the air was completely odorless—and in that heat too. Heat will usually stir up some kind of smell—a faint exudation from the vegetation, a hint of pollenous dust in the air, the odor of stone and earth itself if nothing else—but there was nothing. And there was a breeze, too. Why didn't it pick up something? Because it wasn't really a breeze. It was a huge mass of air moving slowly from one quarter of the world to another. Odorless. It was unnatural. The flautist went on playing his plaintive tune. And I, sitting in that invariable mass of moving air, felt like an old fatalist. The Sun rises and drinks blood. The Sun falls, and the Four Hundred Warriors of the starry sky arise and guard their Mother Moon. The wind circles the earth. The summer rain pits the dust. The small corn tassels and makes a flaxen noise at night. And the Sun also rises. I smiled wryly at myself. It was time to open my eyes, look up. We Americans are not fatalists but climbers and conquerors, sons of Cortez and not of Moctezuma. So if I had stayed behind this time to listen to the flautist's mournful tune of old mortality, it was only an interlude. I must up and prepare myself to mount the Pyramid of the Moon. But when I opened my eyes to see where my three conquistadors were, what caught my attention was a butterfly flitting before me in the near distance, with an eerie irregularity—that is to say, sometimes I saw it and sometimes I didn't. I realize that these weird instants of invisibility were the result of the butterfly's getting its wings and body in a thin plane exactly horizontal to my eyes. Also the undulation of the hot air, as well as my Polaroid sunglasses, probably contributed. But I chose to see it as a metaphysical phenomenon—the butterfly flying back and forth across the border of two layers of reality: the now and the . . . what? The eternal present, the perpetual cycle of Sun, Moon, and Stars. Why not? Hadn't Lane told me that the butterfly, was closely associated with Quetzalcoatl—its transformation from worm to creature of gorgeous pennons an apotheosis, resurrection, translation to the skies in fluted, voluted, venusflight? And as if this wacky skein of images wasn't enough, the flautist suddenly said his first and, it turned out, his only word of our association, "Mariposa." Whereupon he immediately began playing allegretto, and I swear the butterfly picked up the beat and flew even more swiftly in and out of whatever it was flying in and out of. I couldn't take it. I got up waving my hands wildly and shouting, "Basta! Basta!" I figured that if I didn't get free of the butterfly I would stumble into an ontological fault like one of Kafka's poor devils and forever wander around in some old city or island thronged with absurdities.

My three companions were half way back down the pyramid, so I trudged over to meet them, somewhat peevishly, because my stomach was growling and because I had the sense of having been excluded from an adventure. "I'm glad you didn't lose our friend, the fluter," my wife said. She looked at me closely. "You look a little peaked. Want some more Pepto Bismol?" She fished the bottle of pink liquid out of her purse and handed it to me. I unscrewed the top and took a couple of swallows of the slimy, minty stuff with the faint redolence of paregoric. That was all I could get down without gagging. I handed it back to her, rubbed my mouth with the back of my hand, belched, and Bogart-like said, "Thanks, doc."

"I forgot to tell you. Don't worry when your stool turns black."

"Why would I worry?"

"Because in other circumstances it might signify internal bleeding."

"Oh."

"You OK, Dad?" said Lane, the exuberance of the successful climb flushing his face. But I knew that his trials were not over. "Sure, I'm OK." So we walked the last couple of hundred yards down the Avenue of the Dead from the Pyramid of the Sun to the Pyramid of the Moon, Mike in the vanguard, not because he wanted plenty of distance between him and the flautist, but because he always had to be in front. He was not proud or self-promoting. He simply had to be first, a human antenna, but a hell of a lousy one for Lane and me, because he would always call back, just as now from the foot of the Pyramid of the Moons, "Hey! It's a cinch. Come on." So he started up and we came behind lifting our knees high to climb those big stone steps. "It's steeper," said Lane, and I should have taken account right then of the hint of a quaver in his voice, but the truth is that I had dropped a little behind and was watching my wife's legs with fascination. Nothing erotic. On the contrary, I was noting that, though a half a foot shorter than I, she was taking the steps more easily. Obviously she had more spring in her feet, more power in her knees, and twice as much flex in her pelvis, the whole apparatus apparently very rubbery—whereas I felt like I was doing the splits, suffering some kind of male episiotomy. So I said, "According to the original canons of the use of these structures, women were not permitted up here. That's why you're finding the climb a little strenuous."

"No doubt," she said. But Lane corrected me. "In the old days," he said, "there was probably a wooden god house up on the top, and women adjutants to the priests may have had minor offices."

"That's a consolation," my wife said, pulling a little farther ahead of us.

"I thought the highest the women got was to be sorceresses or occasional sacrificial victims by strangulation," I said panting.

"You're thinking of the Aztecs," Lane said.

I was weak, dizzy and a little nauseous, so it didn't occur to me to try to distract Lane from the vertigo he was bound to suffer on those steep steps. In fact, when we reached the middle platform of the pyramid, I looked back down where we had climbed, breathed deep, and said, "Jesus Christ! You guys already scaled one of these monsters and are stupid enough to do another one."

"It's steeper," said Lane, this time his voice weaker, his face grayer. But I didn't take note of these important changes. In my minor sickness I was busy rebelling against my wife and Mike, especially in view of what they were doing at that moment. Mike was restlessly pacing the perimeter of the platform as though this paltry plane of the middle air was too low, too confining for his vaunting spirit—a regular Manfred. And my wife was ecstatically taking in great gulps of air as though she had mounted to some clime of vast spiritual refresh-ment. My irritation with all this superabundant health prevented me from seeing how fearfully Lane sought the middle of the platform, as far as possible from all vertiginous edges. "Tired, old timer?" I said, still missing the mark by a mile. In fact, at this moment I found Lane's weakness as irritating as Mike's and my wife's vigor, mirroring, as it did, my own.

Consequently, when Mike lifted his arm, pointed up the final flight of stones, and shouted "¡Arriba!" I gave Lane a rough slap on the back. "Arriba, the man says."

I don't remember much about the top of the Pyramid of the Moon. No doubt it was more or less flat and at the same time rubblous and wind-gnawed. No doubt it had the inevitable grass or saxifrage growing in crannies between stones—the kind of stuff that is supposed to make the traveler marvel at the mysterious ubiquity of green life. In fact, I think my wife remarked on precisely this matter of unaccountable verdure, and I said, "Bird shit," although I could not myself have been thoroughly convinced of that explanation because I hadn't seen a bird all day, hadn't heard one. I remember then hearing the flautist again. He was below, on the middle level, playing a mournful tune. I remember that Mike scrabbled around and found a chip of obsidian, a piece, he instantly concluded, of an ancient sacrificial knife. Lane had sat down in the middle and was looking at nothing in particular. I gazed down along the Avenue of the Dead to the far end of the ruinous city where I could see the museum, the restaurant, and the parking lot, which spoiled the profound antiquity of my Pisgah view. I was about to call back to my wife peevish observation of that fact, when suddenly I heard behind me a squeal, a grunt, and the sound of scuffling. I turned to find my wife lying on top Lane not far from the edge, his limbs thrashing beneath her weakly. I rushed over. Mike rushed over. My wife said,

"Vertigo. He got up to look over the edge and started teetering."

Almost instantly Lane stopped thrashing. I pushed my wife roughly aside, and Mike and I pulled the now unconscious Lane back away from the edge. I kneeled over him. His breathing was uneven and his face ashen. "Prop up his knees," I instructed Mike while I chaffed his temples. The truth is that I had no real knowledge of the efficacy of these procedures, but I needed desperately to be doing something because I was filled with anger and shame—my wife alone had stood between Lane and death while I had not been vigilant, had not even been thinking of him. And my wife, I'm sure, was wise enough to see my need. How else explain her patiently standing aside at this point? At any rate, I was greatly consoled when at last Lane came to and looked up at me, but the fear in his eyes undercut the consolation. Weakly he began to speak. "I can't . . ." His voice trailed off. But I divined his meaning immediately. "Don't even think about it," I said. "You don't have to climb back down. You don't even have to look." Lane first registered pained disbelief. Probably he thought I was merely telling comforting lies. But his desire to be relieved of the prospect of the dizzying descent was so intense that he necessarily seized on my words and gave them his faith. As a result, he relaxed and began to regain a little color.

Meanwhile, Mike and my wife eyed me with disapproval, believing that I was using false hopes to quiet Lane down. So, when I next spoke I made sure that my voice carried authority. "We'll need your skirt, dear." My wife hesitated, not out of misplaced modesty of course, but because she did not for a moment understand my intention. And during that brief interval we heard the flautist's mournful music rising brokenly up to us against the stones and the wind. "For a litter," I said. "It's good stout denim, right?" She nodded. The skirt was one of those wrap-around things made of the same material they make kids' jeans out of, tough stuff. Still, my wife hesitated, probably this time questioning the feasibility of my plan. "Go ahead, dear. Take it off," I said gently. "Mike and I have a good grip. And you'll lie very quietly, won't you, Lane?" He nodded. There was perhaps even a wisp of a smile playing in the corner of his mouth.

My wife stood up, untied the belt, unfurled the skirt, and took it off. It made something of the same motion as a matador's cape. It wimpled in the wind. In the ring the matador's assistants would hasten to wet it down, for nothing is more dangerous than a wind-blown cape. These irrelevant analogies passed quickly, leaving me peering stupidly at the black shadow of my wife's mons veneris under the sheer cover of her panties. Mike peered too long also before he turned his glance aside. Lane looked up steadily—and though I did not think that his age and innocence really did permit him that indulgence, I didn't rebuke him on this occasion. Fortunately my wife paid no attention to our staring. "All right," she said and spread the skirt out on the stone beside Lane. "Hem at the head and waist at the feet, right?"

"Right. Here's how we'll work it. We'll wrap him up tight. Mike takes the feet, I take the head. You go down right in front of us, backwards, just in case." Actually I should have put Mike at the head, the heavier end, but I wasn't ready to admit that my fifteen-year-old son was stronger and better balanced than I. So we rolled Lane up snug, from shoulder to knee. My wife smiled and said, "What will hatch from our little cocoon?" Her tone was tender, but touched with irony at that—as how could it fail to be, given the comical disabilities of us men?

Mike and I heaved up our burden, awkward but not heavy. "Give it a good shake," I said. "If it's going to rip, we want to find out now, not later." So we tugged on the skirt and gave Lane a good jostling. The cloth proved stout. We carried our burden to the edge and started down. My wife descended two steps ahead of us, backwards, keeping her weight against the steps. That was a great comfort to me, because I began to feel a little queasy. I even considered suggesting that she take the litter and let me be the emergency man, because I knew that this was no place for foolish pride. So if I had continued to feel wavery on those first steps down I would have called on her strength. But quickly I began to get the feel of the litter, picking up the rhythm from Mike, who coordinated our steps with the short swing of Lane's body.

So my crisis of confidence passed. In fact, about half way down to the middle platform I turned my attention to Lane's face. He lay perfectly still in the litter, his eyes shut, his expression a paradoxical cross between deep placidity and repressed terror. I essayed a joke. "I hope, dear, that the God of the Moon will receive the homage of your white buttocks flashing in the mid-morning sun and not tumble us down."

"God of the Moon? Can that be, Lane?" my wife said.

"Goddess," he whispered sibilantly, like one in a trance. "Tlazolteotl, eater of filth, purifier of sinful man."

I started laughing. I couldn't help it. I had to stop and let the litter rest on the stones, which irritated Mike because he couldn't see any humor in what Lane had said. I didn't hold it against him. All the great warriors of the Jaguar and the Eagle were grim, humorless types. I said to my wife, "Not a scrap of consolation for you bloody women's libbers in the mythology of these ancient Mexicans."

"Keep moving," she said. So I stopped my laughter and heaved up my load again. Below, along the Avenue of the Dead groups of bus-borne tourists were just beginning to make their way toward us. I considered how sagacious we had been to come early. Otherwise, in our present predicament we would have had the curious and prurient to contend with.

Down we went. On the middle platform waited the flautist, his face as blank as the stones of the pyramid, his music unchangingly mournful, as though there were absolutely nothing unusual in the manner of our passing. I said, "What a sense of show biz this guy has. If we had all stripped to the skin and come down in the form of a human pyramid, like the kids at Muscle Beach, he would have just kept playing that three-note dirge of his." Mike, as I said, did not appreciate these sallies of humor. I suppose they detracted from the seriousness of the manly business of carrying one's younger brother to safety. But for me, funny or not, they kept vertigo at bay.

"Keep moving," said my wife. So we commenced the descent of the last long flight to the ground, the flautist behind, sending down his constant plaint.

On level ground at last, we laid Lane down in the dust. And then my wife suffered an enormous shiver, of terror just past. I think I've never seen anything quite like it. It seized her shoulders and gave them a violent shake. It curled her lips back from her teeth and momentarily palsied her head. I thought her legs would buckle. And then it passed, almost instantaneously. She stepped toward Lane. "Get out of my way," she said. So Mike and I moved back. She stooped and unwound the skirt, lifted Lane up, and held him to her. He put his arms around her. Surprisingly neither wept. In fact, there was not so much as a snuffle, a tell tale hitch in their breathing. So I didn't feel I would be a callous interloper if I spoke. "You were right, dear. You did snatch him back from the edge. I apologize for doubting you."

She didn't reply. I said, "Maybe you ought to put on your skirt, dear. Here come some British tourists." About two dozen of them, and I didn't need to be a master of fine observation to identify their nationality—pink-faced men with pipes, women in pumps with carious smiles. My wife stood up with Lane, paused a moment to make sure he was steady on his feet, then gathered up her skirt and wrapped it around her. Meanwhile I motioned to the flautist, swaying as he approached. "Bien hecho, bueno y confiable serviente." Well done, good and faithful servant was what I meant. I pulled out my wallet. "¿Cuanto cuesta una flauta?" I said.

"Quarenta pesos." So I gave him two hundred. "Quatro, y el otro quarenta es para un marcho por la Avenida de los Muertos." I motioned with my hand and arm to show him that we would march straight back to the museum. "Hasta el museo." He nodded and pulled out of his little sack four pipes. I gave one each to wife and children with the flourish of an Italian circus impresario. "El Señor Lane en frente," I said, stationing him at the head of our column. "Despues, el Señor Miguel." Mike took the pipe but gave me a deeply suspicious glance. "Be ready to play and march on signal," I said in a momentarily changed voice that left no room for argument. "Despues, la Señora." My wife fell into line smiling. "Despues, el flautista profesional." The Mexican took his place. I brought up the rear. "¡Tocamos! ¡Vamanos!" The Mexican sounded the first note for us. Lane quickly stepped off tooting vigorously. We were on our way. Such a gay cacophony you never heard. The British tourists broke apart like the Red Sea. And we all marched toward the promised land of Lane's manhood.

"Who is this Coatlicue?" I whisper to Lane just as the lights begin to dim for the Finale.

"Coatl—serpent, cue—skirt. Earth Goddess."

"Interesting," I say, but I am thinking, snakes again. All these phalluses, Mexican macho.

"Guess what," says Lane. "I just figured out who the guy with the flute was yesterday."

"Pan."

"Nope. A pochteca, combination of traveling salesman and missionary of Quetzalcoatl."

"Ah," I say. "That explains how he conjured up a butterfly in mid-air and then made it disappear." Lane looks at me and starts to say something, but the curtains are parting and my wife is shushing us.

The stage lies in utter silence and darkness, the primordial void, I suppose. Presently a tiny screed of premonitory fluting creeps out from the pit. "Hey," I say, "they got our boy in the orchestra."

"Sshh!"

Slowly a grayish light seeps down from the flies to reveal in the middle of the stage a huge bicephalic mass. The thing is composed of dancers all twined together, standing on each other's thighs and shoulders, roughly in the shape of a pyramid. The two at the top wear serpent masks with long curving teeth. They seem to be trying to kiss. The rest is a congeries of coiled limbs which the eye cannot untangle except that at the breast bone there is the image of a huge heart and around the heart a fan of human hands. It is these that move first, stroking the heart, coaxing into life the great pump that will send vital blood out into Creation. The action of the hands increases in tempo, in erotic importunity until at last the heart (the artfully masked head of a dancer) begins to beat. Drums in the pit rise rapidly to a thunderous crescendo, at which moment the strange goddess bursts apart. The dancers that once were her fling themselves out into a sudden green light that obviously signifies the greening of the earth. There are, it turns out, a dozen of these living fragments of old earth undulating in the verdant light like creatures of the Ur-slime—tadpoles, spermatozoa. Now other dancers come out from the wings and meet the original fragments. The stage is animated, peopled. And what an incredible facility the dancers have for representing various forms of life. The eye can hardly keep up with all the transformations. We distinguish turtles and dolphins, eagles and butterflies, elephants, tigers, and coyotes, monkeys and men, and much more.

The audience cannot contain itself. Loosed from the ordinary bonds of decorum by these images of irrepressible vitality and by the wild improvisational pizzicato of the orchestra, we begin to shout and clap. But our joy is short-lived. The pizzicato rapidly gives way to a sibylline scraping of the strings. The multicolored lights sink into a crepuscular gray. The variegated dancers vanish. And then slowly the light contracts into the center of the stage, where a skull appears, larger than a Greek tragic mask. No doubt it is atop a tall dancer, but to us it seems to float in mid-air. Presently, like a lodestone, it begins to draw the dancers out of the dark. They come to the center and gather behind the grim memento mori. They climb each other and twine as before. Within moments all is still again—the stony pyramid with its twin serpent head, its serpent skirt, its breastbone of hands and heart—all as before except that this time there is the death's-head. The plaintive flute gives a final call. All is silent, gray, monolithic. Slowly the light fails. The stage is dark. We hear the rustle of the closing curtain. Hesitantly at first, still in deep darkness, we begin to applaud. But quickly we clap louder and louder. The house lights go up. Some of us begin to stand and shout ole! The curtain parts to reveal the entire company, all some-how miraculously changed into simple black. The applause and shouting is thunderous. There are three curtain calls. In addition, the orchestra gets the spot, stands, and takes a bow. Finally the applause dies and the performers are permitted to depart toward a well deserved rest.

As so often after a moving performance, we do not know how to make the transition back to ordinary life. We have trouble putting away these unusual feelings. Our hearts, dilated by the dance, and our eyes, dilated by the dark, are equally vulnerable.

So I take it upon myself to be the clown. "Well, so much for happy endings." No one pays any attention to what I say, but the breaking of silence allows Lane to speak. "Heart and hands are the mandala, the quincunx. And at the omphalos the skull and the navel are the same."

"That says it all," I say, still clowning, but I think I do in fact see what he means.

"Tomorrow back to the good ol' USA," says my wife tugging Mike affectionately on the shoulder. She sees, as I insufficiently have, that this has been perhaps a little too much Lane's day. Furthermore, the program was arranged all wrong for Mike, beginning with the wonders of Ball Game and Sacrifice and then dwindling down to feathers, flowers, serpents, and earth mothers. And even Jaguars and Eagles have feelings. But Mike smiles. He's OK. And Lane of course is marvelously set up by the dance—high as a mountain.

And I? I am dreaming back to Teotihuacan. In one timeless moment I see my wife's beautiful bare legs there on top the Pyramid of the Moon. I see those same strong legs and tight buttocks going down before me. I see her unwrapping and hugging our son Lane. I see her marching in my comic victory parade down the Avenue of the Dead. That is my moment, snatched out of the gray wind that blows forever over the ruined City of the Gods.

THE CASITA

They were playing Do You Remember? sitting over the bones of their steaks, finishing a bottle of Borola that he had found in the neighborhood liquor store. They'd had a pitcher of martinis before supper and so they were a little tight, which was not unusual in the two months since their twins Melissa and Frank had gone off to college. It was windy November. The yard was filling up with maple and birch leaves. But the Barola was rich and bosky. They were remembering scenes from their honeymoon in Italy twenty years ago-a sunny day on the Capri boat with an accordionist and a couple of fiddlers playing on the after deck; a carriage ride up the hill from Florence to a piazza that overlooked the city, amber in the failing sun, and where a replica of Michelangelo's David caught a lovely orange on its marble flesh; and later, from some other prospect, the vision of a man, a boy, and a dog in silhouette out on a rock, the man casting into the Arno. All their honeymoon it was sunny except for one day in Venice when clouds burst over the bell tower in St. Mark's Square and rain pelted the stone and drove the famous pigeons to roost. But even that was fun, having an excuse to sit and drink wine all afternoon and watch the rain stream down the glass. So they went on sharing recollections until suddenly a dark shadow crossed his mind, as though something had flown between him and the light. This had happened before.

"What's the matter?" she said.

"I don't know. Maybe a slightly too liberal partaking of the grape."

She waved that aside. "An unpleasant memory?"

"The shadow of one, or at least the shadow of something."

"Well, there were a number of unpleasant things."

"Really? Name one."

"How about on the way back from Pitti Palace running across that dark door-with the sign above that said Dostoevsky wrote The Idiot there?"

He nodded. "Yes, but it wasn't that."

"What about the cripple who played the mandolin below the balcony of our hotel in Naples, and then hoisted his little basket up under a gas-filled balloon for payment?"

"Why was that a bad memory? Surely the poor bastard needed money."

"It wasn't the money. It was the mocking look he gave us, and the way he played the mandolin, with that evil little plink-plink. He hated us."

"I see what you mean," he said, "but it wasn't that. I think it was something not in Italy."

"Why the hell would you think of something not in Italy? We were remembering our honeymoon." She lit a cigarette. This was also something that had started since the twins left, a cigarette after each meal, which annoyed him because he couldn't do it. One cigarette-maybe just one drag-would plunge him back into the throes of nicotine addiction. It was the twins, of course, who had made them stop in the first place, bringing home from school statistics and pictures of blackened lungs and talking about the rights of non-smokers. He flared his nostrils and said, "I'm remembering the good smokes I had in Italy, like the one leaning over the wall at the potter's place in Sorrento and looking down into the sea and you saying, 'Isn't it marvelous, dear. This is the very sea that Cleopatra bathed in.' "

She blew out a great gust of smoke, alternating it between mouth and nose, a little dragonishly, he thought. Then she said, "No dear, I want you to dredge up this other ugly memory for us."

He didn't say anything for a while. The whole business of smoking and stopping smoking had made him think of the twins. Their absence when he stepped through the front door after work affected him physically. He seemed to yaw and knock around as if the interior of the house were stretched and tilted. Also, the presence of his wife was now enormous, creating a huge pull into whatever room she occupied, usually the kitchen. "Is that you, dear?" And there she would be, waiting for him with wide arms and hungry lips. He said, "Maybe it wasn't a memory at all but just the absence of the kids."

"No," she said, "it was a memory, because we have been remembering."

She was right of course. It was a memory. But he went on with his thoughts of the twins. Why did he miss them so much? He could remember only recently imagining with deep longing what it would be like when they were gone, taking with them their strident quarreling, their endless bitching about household chores, their Brobdingnagian appetites and table manners, their execrable music, their tittering midnight returns with eyes red-rimmed by marijuana (smoking marijuana was totally unrelated to smoking tobacco in their ethic), etc. Was it just the absence of agitation, then, that he missed? No, that was too cynical. And yet he couldn't pretend to any profound love for them. They were too unformed-especially Melissa, blown by every wind of style and doctrine. You couldn't profoundly love a thing that was still so intensely becoming, a veritable chrysalis. But just there in his thinking he stumbled across the real reason for his missing them so. He couldn't watch them taking shape anymore, couldn't try to guess what they were going to become. It left a great deal of his mental equipment idle-idle but not still, with the result that it cranked away making odd images of house, self, wife.

"What's the memory?" said his wife. "Where was it?" And when he had no ready answer, she began a catalogue, "Norfolk, Charleston, Ann Arbor, Seattle, Oxford, London, Paris, Morocco, Seattle, Mexico?"

He smiled. She made it sound as though they were world travelers, whereas in fact they had only been to Europe twice, once on their honeymoon twenty years ago and once two summers ago. And Mexico last spring hardly counted, but Mexico was it, the site of the memory that had cast its dark shadow, a little seacoast resort called Zanatlan. "Where?" said his wife.

"Mexico."

"Zanatlan?"

He nodded. She said, "Well, why don't you tell me about it, get it out of your system."

So he told the story, she occasionally making inquisitorial interruptions.

Once upon a time a man and his wife and two children met a very nice lady in Guadalajara who said, "¿Porque no visitan ustedes mi casita en la playa?" (Why not visit my cottage on the beach?) There would be no charge because the nice lady wanted to sell the cottage and frankly it would be to her benefit to have some moneyed Norteamericanos stay there and spread the word.

"Did everyone think she was a nice lady at the time of this unusual offer?"

The wife was suspicious. She thought she detected anti-Americanism, malice, but the children and the husband were enthusiastic, so they took the key and a hand-sketched map from the kind lady and bought tickets on the famous Mexican bus line Flecha Amarilla.

"Tres Estrellas."

They took the Three Stars bus over the mountains, through the jungle city of Colima, and around the volcano to the quaint village of Zanatlan by the sea, a trip of some six hours, half of which, it seemed to the husband, was spent under the louring influence of the volcano. He noted that the volcano smoked continuously and that at sunset the slant light caught in the cloudy effluent what looked like a message in a curious scrolling hand which he could not decipher. Mentioning this to his son, he was quickly illuminated. "It's just a warning sign, Dad. It says Peligro. Danger."

At 11 p.m. the bus deposited the four of them on a corner under a yellow streetlight that was swarming with long silver-winged bugs, so many of them that their flying made a scraping sound like the edge of a knife on a whetstone. Examining the kind lady's map, beating the bugs from their heads, they quickly decided on a direction and began tramping up a sand road. The sand was so fine and deep that it sucked the sandals off the wife's feet. And while they were stopped so that she could replace them, two things occurred. First they heard in the near distance the rumble of breaking sea, which had been obscured until that moment by the buzzing of the bugs and the slogging sound of their feet in the sand. Second, they saw looming up from the far perimeter of the streetlight's reach two drunk Mexicans, arms on each other's shoulders, who approached forthwith and stood before them, weaving and smiling, one with an amused solicitude, the other blankly. He was retarded. "¿Quieren un hotel señores?" said the normal one.

The daughter, whose Spanish was excellent, made reply. No thanks, they were looking for the cottage of Señora Moreno y Lares, which, according to the map, ought to be close by. Could the kind gentleman offer assistance?

Well now, this called for special consideration. The normal drunk disengaged himself from his friend the idiot, mumbling all the while "Moreno y Lares, Moreno y Lares," a name which his alcohol-clouded memory did not easily recover. To aid in the ruminative effort he fished a cigarette from his shirt pocket and lit it, and then, suddenly aware of his lapse in etiquette, offered the pack around with a flourish. All refused except, to the murmuring horror of her kinspersons, the wife. She took a cigarette and tucked it behind her ear. This merely amused the normal drunk but utterly destroyed his friend the idiot, who began to chortle and hiccup in a seizure of mirth that finally drove him to his knees weeping and slobbering on the sand. "Pobre Vicente," said the normal drunk.

"And did they finally get to the casita?"

Yes, winning at last from the reluctant drunk (who still recommended a hotel) directions to the cottage of Señora Moreno y Lares, the family proceeded there with alacrity, and the eager son unlocked the door. The son also recalled the directions for finding the electrical switch box in the kitchen. The father lit a match, found candles and accompanied the son, but the box was a Medusa's head of copper coils and neither of them dared touch it. Back in the little living room they found another candle in a sconce on the wall and lit it.

"And what did the wife do?"

The wife sat in a wicker chair and smoked the cigarette the drunk Mexican had given her and dared any of the proponents of this visit to the casita of Señora Moreno y Lares to say a word to her about the evils of tobacco. So the three of them went off to explore the house by candlelight. Upstairs they found two bedrooms, each with a lumpish double bed, mattresses covered by disheveled sheets, and so strong an odor of bodies that they shrank back into the hall for fear that angry sleepers had been awakened by their entry and lurked in dark corners. Downstairs again, they spotted in the kitchen sink two huge hairy spiders, one scrambling awkwardly on top the other in fumbling attempt at copulation.

Back in the living room, they found the air pleasantly spiced with that same tobacco smoke which had so often been the subject of bitter complaint.

"What was the wife doing?"

The wife was looking up at a prehistoric lizard slowly making its way on suction-cup toes across the ceiling. She said, "If that thing loses its grip and falls in my lap. . ." Fortunately it did not. All four grew very quiet. The sounds of the night came flowing back to them-the rumble of the sea rising and falling, the clatter of dry palm leaves, the high call of a single night bird, and finally a tiny splashing sound from the kitchen. "What's that?" said the daughter.

"Take the candle and go see," said the son. But the daughter didn't move, so the husband went. What he found was a tiny mouse-like creature swimming violently in a garrafon, a big glass jug slung in a tiltable metal stand. It had once held purified water, but the top was off and the water was now discolored by dust and perhaps by the excretions of the terrified little beast. The husband found a long broom straw and extended it down to the creature, but the straw only frightened it and sent it swimming even more wildly around the edge of the glass.

The husband found an old kitchen towel, stripped a piece off, and carefully lowered it down. But the little animal kept swimming madly in circles. So, reluctantly, with a sinking feeling, the husband gave up his life-saving operation.

Back in the living room he said, "A shrew or something drowning in the garrafon."

The wife said, "Hotel?"

They found a nice hotel. Their room had a balcony overlooking the beach. Rich salt air flowed through all day and night. The sea was a deep green except for the breakers, which were chartreuse. The sand was brown and the sky a constant blue. It was like no other seascape they had ever seen.

"Did they have a good time?"

Oh yes, they enjoyed their stay on the beach, drinking coconut milk laced with gin, eating melons and shrimp and langostino and strange custardy ice cream pressed from metal tubes. One afternoon some Mexican kids took the twins on a sailboat ride out beyond the breakers where they drank beer and sang to a guitar. The husband and the wife closed the curtains of the room and made love.

"Purged?" she said.

He nodded, but he was far from purged. He remembered how that first night in the hotel he had awakened with the sound of water in his ears-not the thunderous ocean but the plash of the drowning animal. It had come to him in his sleep how simple it would have been to save it. All he had to do was tilt the garrafon down and pour the water out on the floor. The little creature would tumble out and dash away to freedom. So he wanted to jump up out of his bed and run back to the casita, but he couldn't do it. It was too foolish, too emotionally errant. So he lay there the rest of the night breathing in the thick salt air, crying out in the deep recesses of his psyche, drowning, drowning. While all around him the noises of the world went on: the unmusical breathing of other humans, the silver scraping of bugs, the undulant roar of the sea, the night birds' strident calls, and in the tiny interstices of all these, the brushy whisper of spider love.

"I'll clean up," she said.

I'll help."

The problem now was how to get free of memory and into a clear enough space for desire to ignite. That, of course, was the goal of the long ritual of martinis, red meat, and red wine. But he was still in Zanatlan. He was remembering how he planned to slip away the next day on some pretext and go back to the casita. He wanted to see in the bright daylight the images of the night before and reduce them to normal proportions. More important, he wanted to fish the dead creature out of the garrafon and thus, by his concern, by his touch, remove the recriminations of disregard. But he didn't. On the sunny beach even a casual stroll back to the casita seemed silly, mildly neurotic. Maybe he would go the next day. But that afternoon, looking through her purse for change for another gin coconut, his wife ran across the key to the casita and said, "Here, Frank, take this and throw it into the ocean."

"We're supposed to leave it at the Cafe Sol," he said, trying to grab the key away from his wife. But she laughed raucously and thrust it into Frank's hand. "Throw it, dammit. Throw Señora Moreno y Lares' key in the ocean."

So Frank and Melissa ran laughing into the surf and jettisoned the key.

How was he to know then that he had doomed himself to return to the casita in memory ever and again, like a murderer to the scene of the crime? And even when he was not consciously revisiting the casita, still the spiders, the lizards and the drowning beast scratched on the undersurface of his mind. And as a result he was doomed to lose his wife, had already all but lost her, through mental and emotional absence. The steak bones were cold. The sauce of butter, rosemary, and lemon was congealed on the plates. The trees were going bare. The marriage bed was cold.

"What are you going to do now?" he asked after the kitchen was done.

"Oh, watch TV for a while I guess." She was not bitter, as he feared she might be. Actually her voice was mild, almost forgiving.

"I'll sit with you and look at the paper." But what he actually looked at was the images in the window behind the TV, the dark outline of swaying trees. Soon the backyard would fill up with snow, which reminded him of a very strange story he had once read-about an old man on an endless voyage into winter because of some chink in vigilance, the omission of some minor rite of love.

A CHILD OF FIRE

We have come to this long island, my wife and I, in its most variable season. How will we learn to interpret its small signs? Some advised that we plunge ourselves into healing routines—counsel we did not take. We have opted for revelation, not forgetfulness. To the destructive element submit. Come through burned but alive.

I know that my wife has dreamed of attacking me, tearing my face until the eyes are shadeless wounds and the lipless mouth a perpetual O of penitence. Repent ye. Repent ye. Of what? Was not the net of my paternal love woven with extraordinary care? And yet, I concede, our daughter slipped through and is gone, into the deepest dark.

Well, all is balanced here on the island. I too have a brutal dream, in which I beat my wife until she is blue, until the blood clots her heart as the deep sea congeals around the roots of this island. Of course she is no guiltier than I. But we men believe a mother's love ought to be perfect. Consider the Pieta. Mary has not lost her son. Despite the politicians, the rabble, the impossibly high calling, she has him still, holds him in her lap. But our daughter is gone utterly, not so much as a lock of hair left to us. How can love fail so utterly?

Underneath the floor of our rented cottage an April bug ticks, not like a clock or a bomb. Ticks a pure insect tick. Flicks a metallic pincer against its carapace. "What do you think he wants?" my wife says.

"Wants? Insects don't want. They behave mechanically, according to pre-set biograms. And what makes you think it's a he?"

"If he had his mate he would stop ticking."

Arguments, even as seemingly innocent as this, are dangerous. I say, "I expect you're right."

Our sub floor ticker is absolutely unpredictable—ticks night or day, ticks long or short, ticks strident, desperate, ticks faintly, wearily. But the rest of the insects of the island are more regular. At nightfall their voices rise up out of the sand and the rough brush with a furious intensity. By midnight, though, very few carry on, and they are a fearful lot. If I clap my hands, they keep silence a long minute.

Neither of us can identify anything beyond the crickets and the katydids of all those hundreds of buzzers and chirpers and brackers and trillers. But we easily agree on our favorite, a Doppler bug that comes whirring up at us with tremendous velocity and then fades down a low buzz. I say, "What if it really is what it sounds like, an insect from outer space? No entomologist has ever seen it.

Streaming from an unknown source toward an unknown destiny, it shares with us only one instant of its flight." I mean to lighten our mood with this distended poeticizing. But foolishly, driven perhaps—God knows—by unconscious impulse, I have stumbled into the one half of a perilous analogy. We listen to the insects in silence. Still, we know the revelation approaches. It is why we are here.

I have been the confidant of two friends who went through painful divorces. One, morose, merely wanted a friendly presence. A dog would have done. But the other was informative. He recounted for me the growth of loathing, a phenomenon common enough, I suppose, but unfamiliar to me. He told me how his wife's hair got ratty and gave off an odor like a cat-stained rug. Her ears, he noticed, were waxy and bitter to the tongue. Her face deteriorated markedly with drink—the eyes drooped, the nose flared piggishly, and the mouth went slack. He discovered that her body was porous and punky . . . and there were details of even deeper revulsion, but why go on? I introduce the matter here as a contrast. Though I would like to beat my wife's body blue, it has never for one moment lost its familiar fragrance. No, we're not talking here about mere estrangement, the decay of love, corporal revulsion, etc. We're talking about the relentless gall, indescribably corrosive, of loss, loss of an only child, a wondrous flaming tulip tree of a child. And not just the child on the brink of young womanhood, as she was when she left us, but the child in all the stages of acquisition from infancy through adolescence—the arts of movement and speech, the discipline of finger and eye to inquiry, the stylization of adornment and desire, and so on. Not a hair remaining, not a wayward snapshot (these all carefully gathered from friends before the act) not even an old pillow or doll with the redolence of her touch.

"Where is the school picture you kept in your wallet?" my wife asked.

"I don't know."

How can it be that we have no scrap of evidence of her existence outside the fierce accusation of our own eyes?

My wife has taken up with the gulls, throws them scraps from our little porch out onto the sand in front of the cottage. "It's egg-laying time," she says. "They need extra food." I try to discourage her. I tell her that toward the end of the Age of Man, when we have despoiled all nature and are choking to death in our own offal, we still will have a trinity of boon companions—rats, gulls, and carp—thieves, scavengers, and bottom feeders. But yesterday one of the gulls took station outside our bedroom window and hovered lovely there in the wind. A windhover, I know, is a fine accipiter, nothing like these fat white beasts. But this particular gull had a piercing red eye that fixed me. My wife saw it too. We were lying together on our cold marriage bed, reading. So I considered that maybe the gull was Love's detective spying out our misprisions. Presently he tipped his wings and wheeled away to make report of the death we courted.

"The end of the Age of Man?" my wife says. "I thought you said that man would transform himself, that the bio-geneticists would tell us how to make ourselves better and those better in turn would create still better and on and on." What has begun as only a reminder of my inconsistency now verges on mockery. But there is no danger of reprisal from me, because I not only remember mouthing that foolishness but remember the impulse behind it. Which at the time seemed a wondrous marriage of logic and vision. To wit, if there was grace like my daughter's, might it not be plucked out of those old evolutionary excrescences, isolated by artful manipulation of heredity, and thus established as our quintessential quality? How was I to know that my daughter would take herself away and leave the species without its model of grace?

"Well?" says my wife.

I cannot answer. Tears scarify my cheeks. "That's what you wanted," I blubber. She leaves me alone.

Let me describe for you a midnight confusion of fire and water. To begin factually, there was no fire left when my wife and I arrived at the scene. There was a column of dense smoke. There was a platoon of helmeted and slickered firemen rolling up two long hoses. There were a half dozen curious bystanders from the two farms downhill, our only near neighbors. They shrank back, not wishing to speak to us. Who can blame them? Everyone knew that more than house and chattels had perished in the fire. And in my mind's eye I saw our beloved A-frame crowned and tippeted by flame like a priceless miter. And there on the second floor, crosspiece of the A, was the white-hot image of our daughter, the very heart of the fire. I turned to my wife, thinking she would see in my eye the miraculous image of our alpha-house burning, burning into a future beyond our ken. But all she saw was the smoking ruin. Even the basement walls of thick cement had burst asunder in the huge heat so that what was left standing reminded one of a gat-toothed jaw a dog has dug up in a deer field. Anyway, so blackly bereft were my wife's eyes that they shattered my fond image of glorious transfiguration. In fact, when I looked again at the column of slowly failing smoke, it was not rising, but falling, because suddenly the universe was upside down. The sky was a dark sea. And all I loved best now drained away into those black waters. At that moment my wife began to keen like a banshee. I was afraid to touch her. The oldest of the farm wives had to come and hold her until she finally focused her grief enough to begin calling our daughter's name over and over. Margaret, Margaret, Margaret. The grizzled chief of the firemen came by. I think he actually tipped his firefighter's hat, as old gentlemen of the South salute ladies on the street. "All we could do," he said, "was wet down the trees."

The divorcer who delineated for me so vividly the decay of his ex-wife's person is John Quilty, owner of an art gallery, the kind of person I assiduously avoid, but Quilty and his wife lived on the road from town out to our house, had a car that rarely ran, and so he often hooked rides with me in the morning. Before the divorce occupied his thoughts, he began telling me of a vast work of art unfurling in long skeins from the convolutions of his imagination. "This is a collage?" I asked. Somehow I had in mind a huge billboard-like thing plastered with faces, legs, balloons, headlines, that kind of stuff.

"I don't know, man. I don't know." He made a fluttering motion with his hand. "I think it's print media."

"A novel?"

"No. Bigger. Tabloid and panorama, big press stuff."

"What's the subject?" I asked.

"The sixties—on big sheets so people can pick up any piece, like the old broadside ballads, and recite it, chant it, sing it. You keep running it off and putting it out on the street. Groups at noon in central cities get together and sing it."

I found all of this ridiculous, disturbing, moving. I began to envision a scene. Gray dawn breaks over the black streets of a wretched urban neighborhood. A caustic wind gnaws wood and stone. Huge sheets of Quilty's work tumble down the sidewalk. A few ragged urchins and oldsters venture out, no ages between. Some cataclysmic event has annihilated all others. Anyway, these remnants begin to gather up the sheets. I cannot make out the words. I wait for them to congregate and chant. Well, that was as far as I got with my scene because presently the subject became Quilty's divorce. And now, here on the island, I keep all of this out of mind. Otherwise I am likely to remember the incident in which a newspaper reporter asked my wife if she had a picture of Margaret. This cruel request struck her dumb, bringing to the surface what she had known until then only implicitly, that all she would ever have of Margaret was locked in her own brain. And remember, this was before it was disclosed that I had lost my wallet picture and that Margaret had gathered all photos from friends.

I said to the gentleman of the press, "No. We have nothing."

The photo I had in my wallet was a school picture dated 1972, the year before the fire—Margaret age 15. Never did I display it for friend or business associate. Why? Because I was not a normally proud father? No, because it was a picture of nakedness. Though only her head, her neck, and the shoulders of a red sweater were visible, the fact is that the face was painfully naked. Nothing could mar the subject's essential beauty, the lustrous dark eyes, the long curving lashes, and the fine black brows. But the blush was not a blush of pleasure nor a virgin blush. It was a blush born of the pure pain of exposure. I don't mean that the subject wished to remain aloof from her fellow men. On the contrary, she tended to find many of them miraculously beautiful. (Though never island or father-sequestered, a kind of Miranda.) But while she admired, she could not bear to be looked at in turn. Thus, as a child she was a great lover of windows and books, and the combination of the two was paradise—to sit in a window seat and glance from page to street. Not surprisingly then that all of her life she wanted glasses, played with mine, tried them on. I divined her need, and when she entered her troubled period, I suggested lightly that a pair with clear glass might be fun. I favored big round owlish lenses enclosed in black rims.

"Why owlish?" she wanted to know, on guard against a jibe.

"Because the owl is Athena's bird. And you, like Athena, are wise, well read, and deeply thought, beyond your years. I do not speak of beauty, lest I engender vanity. So the spectacles, if not refractive, would be properly symbolic." I was accustomed to clothe my love in pedantry—naked, it would have fawned and slavered. And who knows? Perhaps I had premonition of loss and so protected myself with such little distance as I could acquire.

She shook her head and said, with some regret, "I don't need them." But O my daughter, you did need them, and more, much more than mere glass, to set between your eyes and what was to pass.

Here on the island I want to speak of the beach. The sandpipers attract us, scurrying this way and that, high-stepping, stilt-legged, greeting each incoming wave with such shrill exuberance that one would think the sea a spilling cornucopia. But what, exactly, we ask, are these wonders the sandpipers dip their long beaks to? So we ourselves go barefoot in April down the strand to inspect these munificent waves. The sun is bright and passably warm down here in the south. It's comforting to know that old earth is wobbling its regular way toward the hot months. Well, unfortunately our friends the pipers scold us, give us wide berth, and keep their feast at a distance. "How do you know they're eating?" asks my wife.

"Well, maybe they aren't eating," I say. "Maybe they're oceanographic hobbyists, tidal researchers." There is more sarcasm in my voice than I would like. I have seen the waves wash away my footsteps, and my evanescence angers me. "They're eating things we cannot see. They're eating the very organisms out of which their ancestors eons ago crawled serpent-like onto the shore. The fetus, they say, recapitulates evolution. How nice to be able to eat your own embryo daily." My wife knows that I am over the edge now, stands away from me, crosses her arms under her breasts and waits for the madness to play itself out. I scoop up great fistfuls of shells and pour them back into the sea. It is the inverted image of that dead column of smoke that poured out into the midnight sky. I say, "This is the vastest graveyard under the sun. In one motion I tumble thousands." I begin to cackle. I have lost control. "Do you think the sea had the likes of us in mind when she was impregnated by the great electrical storms, when her womb swarmed with huge protein molecules? Do you?"

"Stephen!" My wife knows she can't stop me, but by calling my name she may keep something of my true self in view.

"No wonder, for Christ's sake! You never let her see in you anything of our common human evil. You always had to be so Goddam good!" I snivel and puddle about blindly in the sand. "At least, for God's sake, we should have searched the ashes. We might have lucked onto a little bone that had tumbled under a skillet. We could have shined it up and worn it by turns around our necks."

"Stephen! Stephen!"

Quilty found it interesting that his ex and my wife were both named Elizabeth. "But I'm only mildly into synchronicity," he said. Once he invited me into his little house: bongo, cannabis plants under florescent lights, LP's with spacey jackets, posters of sky-piercing pyramids and suns with huge root systems lacing the bowels of earth, esoteric books, the musk of unwashed clothes, etc. "So," I said, "what is your metaphysics?"

"Process," he said.

"You're an evolutionist."

"No, in evolution you got lots of forms all fanned out like a deck of cards in a magician's trick, saying to Mother Nature, pick one, any one. See if you like it. But in Process everything was always potentially there." This was much more learned than I had expected. I asked him how it all fit in with his huge-sheeted work of the 60's. "In the 60's we tried to get off the forms that are anti-Process, like monarchy and federalism. We tried to get movement." Back in the car Quilty lit a cigarette. And I was thinking that the only movement in Quilty's life was toward death—blackening of lungs, fuzzing of brain, killing of marriage, destroying of son, who I had heard was maybe psychopathic. Imagine my horrified surprise, then, to hear Quilty say, "Peter says your daughter Margaret builds him up."

"Where is Peter?"

"Mostly with his mother."

On the beach we encounter the Ancient of Days. We tell him that we are Elizabeth and Stephen Marston, but no more expect exchange of name than we would encountering Chronos scything his way down a steppe of Russia. His blue eyes are deeply recessed, but not rheumy. He finds us by the water's edge, rucking among the shells. I wonder if he can read the hieroglyphs etched in these tiny fragments and tell us what creatures they were in the sunny days when they masoned their spiraling mansions. I wonder if he will divine our sorrow and make some mild movement in the stones about our hearts so that the grief can shoal away. I look forward hopefully to his speech. He reveals that he has lived all his life on the island. My wife says, "Then tell us a famous story of the islands because we are newcomers." I imagine that I see pass behind his eyes many wondrous tales—invasion, smuggling, spying, shipwreck, etc. It is a tale of storm he decides to tell us. "There was nothing ever like it, black as pitch Sunday noon and a sound like the biggest drums ever rolled. And after it broke nothing stood but half the south wall of the old tannery. Nothing to hunker behind but dunes themselves and only the highest of them not washed over by waves. In the morning every piece of wood was so raked and splintered you couldn't tell a rafter from a strake off Elbert's shrimper."

"How many were dead?" I asked, half hoping that he had been the sole survivor.

"Eight were dead, some others bad. A doctor came over in a fancy boat. And a mortician was offered. But we buried our own. And then we commenced to eat oysters."

"Oysters?"

"Yes. The storm tumbled big clumps of oyster beds up on the beach, some as high as houses. So we ate oysters. At night we built fires and cooked oysters. But the sun came out the third day and the oysters began to rot. There was not a cubby of the island where you could get away from the stench. So it was not the human dead but oysters that stuffed our noses. After a while the sun dried the rot up, and a barge came over with food and wood for us to rebuild."

"Good," said my wife.

But I had in my mind's eye great bonfires on the beach, the axle of the sky black with smoke and the rim of stars wavering in the heat. If I had been there, I would have heaped all the bodies onto the fire, heaped rotting oysters onto the fire. Fire, purifying fire, and a ceaseless column of thick smoke to fatten the gods of the midnight sky.

So I went in search of Peter, son of Elizabeth and the Process Philosopher. The mother resided in another cabin on another road out from town—all exits and entrances of our innocent municipality lined with these problematic members of the counterculture. No wonder the good burghers and villagers of old would from time to time march out and fall upon gypsies and witches with incredible fury, burn clean the outlands, the dark precincts of the communal psyche. Quilty was right. The woman stank—an odor not precisely acrid but rife with unclean musk. I could not bear the thought of my daughter consorting with the whelp of this bedraggled bitch. She was accoutremented in the uniform of her kind: granny glasses, lumpish sweater, long skirt pieced together from worn jeans, wooden sandals, etc. Had I been in a crowd of righteous citizenry, I confess I would have eagerly set torch to the gray wood walls of that poor cottage, would have been in the first rank of those who with pikes and poles thrust mother and son screaming back into the flames. But it was not the son I glimpsed beyond the woman at the door. It was a bearded presence that peered at me curiously and then slipped out of sight. The woman narrowed her eyes behind the granny glasses.

"I'm sorry to bother you," I said, "but are you Peter Quilty's mother?"

"Yes."

"May I have a word with you?"

"Yes," she said, but did not invite me in.

"Your son and my daughter are seeing each other. My daughter's name is Margaret Marston. At the moment she is under the care of a psychiatrist, who believes that the relationship between the two kids is aggravating my daughter's illness." It is true that Margaret was seeing a psychiatrist, Dr. Pearl Mueller, but nothing had been said about Peter. Elizabeth Quilty judged it all a lie, I suspect—the concoction of a square citizen who did not want his daughter playing with a hippie kid. "Go on," she said.

"Well, could you speak to Peter, explain the situation, ask him to drop his friendship with my daughter, at least for the time being, for her sake?"

"I think you'd better be the one to do that," she said.

"All right. Is he here?"

"I think he's down at the creek. Take the trail behind the house."

I found Peter at the creek all right, but for a long strange moment I suffered a painful illusion. Kneeling by the creek, back to me, was a naked child with long black hair that fell over the shoulders and cascaded down to the last node of the spine. The child seemed very much like my daughter—the glistening hair, the alabaster-like flesh. What was it that finally broke the illusion? Some hint of pubescent maleness, I suppose. Still, I remember that when I said, "Peter?" my voice quavered uncertainly.

So there were ceremonies at a Unitarian church—recitation of poetry, performance of music, soft speech. I would have preferred the traditional images of grass, dust, the seasons wheeling us towards death, but I didn't oppose my wife. Friends who had never hugged us in life hugged us in death. I was alarmed by the immense heat of their bodies, but submitted with such grace as I could find, knowing what a great comfort it was to my wife. At the end of three days I went in search of a photo.

Two friends there were of my daughter who might have had a picture. I found them together. It was an unhappy meeting. I wore my grief so openly that they shrank from me, edged together on the sofa and held hands. And they were scarcely more pleasing to me, awkward gray goslings left to populate the sunless world from which my resplendent swan of a daughter had departed in a blaze of white hot glory.

"Did she give you a picture?"

One of them nodded, lifting my hopes, until the other added, "She took it back . . . just before."

"Wait." The one that had first spoken went away. And while she was gone I saw again in my mind's eye the bright fire alpha leaping up into the night while far above arched the black dome of the sky, inviolate omega.

"Here." My daughter's friend was standing in front of me, a little fearfully, trying to hand me something, a photo. I took it and looked at it, stupidly. The two who were with me were pictured in a motley wood of fir and birch. Behind them was a pup tent, ill strung, its crest sagging, its sides bowed. "There." An ugly little nail-bitten finger came forward and pointed out a head protruding from the tent. Yes, it was my daughter. I recognized the black hair and the general configuration of the face, but all was fuzzy because the photographer had focused on the gray goslings in the foreground. I took my glasses off and looked yet more closely. My daughter's face was indistinct, eroded—by what? By lack of concentration. But how could that be? At times I had looked so lovingly at her that I thought it improper for a father. So how could this face be gnawed by neglect? I do not even speak of the wreathing love of her mother, who a little later met me at the door and saw the emptiness in my eyes before I spoke it. "They had nothing," I said. "Nothing."

How long did I remain gazing silently at the naked child crouching by the creek? Too long. I should have known better than to blazon that image on my eye. But I stood still, breathing softly, until at last the child, sensing my presences began to turn. "Peter? Peter," I said.

"Yes?"

"Hello. I'm Margaret's father."

"She's not here," he said.

"I know that. But I want to talk to you about her."

He stood up and walked a little apart from me, but there was no question of his running away. Neither was there awkwardness about his nudity. It was as if I had simply found him in his natural state and habitat. He was just pubescent, a light-colored tuft of hair above his small penis, but his chest still clear. Only months ago, I judged, he would have seemed androgynous. But now he was perceptibly male.

"Go ahead," he said, his blue eyes and his small rather pinched face compliant. But I didn't go on, because I had suddenly noticed his right hand. The thumb and the first two fingers were deep yellow, almost amber—tobacco stains of course, but a perverse thought crossed my mind, that these were stigmata caused by his illicitly touching himself, or another. I had to get that out of my mind immediately, so I asked a question. "Are you a forest creature?"

"Do you mean why don't I have any clothes on?"

"Yes, and why do you study the creek like that?"

"It keeps me from sweating and smoking, same as when I'm with Margaret."

The child's utter straightforwardness required of me an equal directness. "What do you smoke?"

"Tobacco. I don't like the effects of grass."

I nodded. "And the sweating. Why do you sweat?"

"I don't know, but when I go to school my hands sweat and my feet sweat. But when I talk to Margaret or come here and take off my clothes and look at the creek, then I don't sweat."

"But you don't do both at the same time."

"What?"

"Take off your clothes and talk to Margaret." He didn't answer but of course I already knew, already saw in my mind's eye the two backs against the creek, the black hair cascading down.

It was inevitable that our futile search for a memento would turn into a quest for causes. It was my wife, we decided, who should talk to Dr. Pearl Mueller—bereaved mother to physician, woman to woman. But when she returned, I couldn't tell from her face how much she had learned, only that it was painful. In answer to my inquisitive look she said, "She was deeply ashamed of all her imperfections." That was the crux of Dr. Mueller's wisdom. Obviously my face remained quizzical. My wife said, "She was especially ashamed of her body."

"Is that all?"

"Remember, Dr. Mueller only had her for three sessions."

"Well, that about the body is an oversimplification."

"How do you know?"

"Because she and Peter Quilty used to disrobe and sit by the creek behind his mother's house."

My wife looked at me closely, "When did you find that out?"

"Maybe a month ago."

"And you didn't tell me?"

"I didn't know how to tell you, didn't know exactly what it meant. And I still don't."

My agonized puzzlement extinguished the anger that had flared momentarily in my wife's face. "Dr. Mueller spoke of Peter Quilty."

"So, you already heard about the nakedness."

"No not exactly."

"What do you mean? What did the doctor say?"

"She said that Margaret and Peter Quilty were drawn together because they tended to function to legitimize their feelings about themselves."

That language, utterly alien in my wife's mouth, irked me. "What the hell is that supposed to mean?"

"Dr. Mueller said that Peter Quilty suffered the same shame as Margaret."

"Don't tell me he was a patient of hers too."

"No. This is the Peter Quilty of Margaret's accounts. Dr. Mueller has never seen him. In fact, at first she thought he was a creature of Margaret's imagination, someone who wouldn't look at her so hard. So they shared their nakedness. They were the only ones they trusted with it."

"Oh quit making Peter Quilty out to be some kind of soul-mate of Margaret's. He was nothing, goddamit, but a sick dirty little hippie kid that she

67

took in like a stray cat." My wife shook her head and reached for my hand, but I drew back, scalded by shame. "Don't touch me."

The ticker under our cabin floor is a time bomb beating toward another moment of white-hot illumination. The villain who set it is me. The sharp-eyed gull that hovers outside the window of the room wherein stands the cold marriage bed reminds me that nothing can be concealed, that on judgment day earth will give up all her secrets. And the pipers on the beach scold me and flee me, a thing corrupted. Nevertheless, though illumination is what we have come here for, I cannot drive myself to it. I'm not ready. But the Doppler bug whizzes and whizzes.

Meanwhile the ancient of the island tells us about the rare Lagniappe, what I think is called elsewhere a Jubilee. "They come to this side," he says, of the fish that swarm into the shallows. I forget the probable causes of this—disorienting fungi, something in the fish world equivalent to earwigs? The old man says, "They're thick all the way down to the jetty." He traces slowly with finger and eye the long reach of the crazed fish. "All the way along here up to where the shore breaks east." Obviously his memory is vivid. And I see the Lagniappe myself—a silver thrashing at the water's edge. The old man smiles. "It's the payback from the hurricanes. The sea giveth and the sea taketh away." He is proud of that and pauses to make sure we take it in before he goes on. "Because then there's mighty good eating, and good profit. We have a Lagniappe flag, and when the buyer sees it on the mainland he brings over a barge. And we harvest and clean 'em. The fish are ours and he must buy."

"What does the Lagniappe flag look like?" my wife asks.

The old man's eyes widen. "It's a long pennant, a hundred feet. Half black and half red, and forked at the tip. It has to be a thing that can't be missed because the buyer must come quick or the fish will rot."

"Red and black," says my wife wonderingly.

"Yes," says the old man with a hint of impatience, "because it must be seen."

As soon as the old man leaves, my wife rushes out into the waves and splashes about. Does she believe that the fish of the Lagniappe have left behind a healing effluent of their vital dying? I don't know. Presently she comes running back, her thighs water-slick. An image comes to me. My daughter is sitting in her window seat reading. Her knees are propped up. Her skirt has fallen half down her lovely thighs. Rainwater wrinkles the pane. Out in the green backyard my wife potters about in slicker and back-billed sou'wester, like a New England fisherman, and smiles up at me through the arch of Margaret's legs—strange image, the child the mother of the woman.

Why was it precisely that I failed to report to my wife that conversation with Peter by the creek? Was it the difficulty of conveying those powerful images: dappled creek, black hair, yellow fingers? Or was it the instinctive fear, even then, that I had done a desperately unwise and shameful thing?

I sat down on a rock. "You know, Peter, I can't remember when I was your age what we talked about, my friends and I. What do you and Margaret talk about?"

He thought about that. He wasn't nervous, didn't sweat or long for a cigarette. There, naked by the creek, he was master of his soul and invulnerable to emissaries, like me, from the world of the school. "I can't tell you what we say. It's between us."

"Oh, I would never ask you what you say. I just wonder what you talk about."

"Lots of the time we don't talk about anything. We just sit and watch the creek," he said. I had the feeling he wanted to add something about a kind of wordless communication that passed between them, through their bodies in part, but such a thing would have been enormously difficult for a child to explain. There was a long silence, and then he said, "Sometimes we talk about people."

"Like?"

"My mother and father."

"And Margaret's mother and father?"

He shook his head. "Or teachers or other kids."

I nodded. I understood how they would come here, safe in their naked-ness and silence, and then break that silence in order to try to weave of words a shield against the raging beasts of humanity outside. How pitiful, the strawy, the child's-play thing they held athwart our advance. I said, "You and Margaret have to stop seeing each other for a while."

"Why?"

"I don't know. Because she's a little sick in her mind and has to see a doctor for it. And these talks with you are too strong for her." His face filled up with grief, but there were no tears. "I promise you," I said, "that when it's all right for her to see you again, I'll let you know. I'll send her right over. But if she tries to come now, you must hide in the woods, for her sake."

A sudden shrewd courage shot unexpectedly into the sorrowful little face. "I can hide so that nobody can find me."

The next time the old man approaches, I make an excuse and go back to the cabins leaving him to talk to my wife. I don't want to hear any more of his tales—of the wind consuming human flesh, of humans consuming fish. Even so, I watch the two of them from the window. My wife looks up at him, rapt. "Beware, Elizabeth," I want to call out. "This is a violent old man, a flesh-eater." I see his mouth moving, full of good teeth. Today, I judge, he is telling a story about something in the deep. He frightens me.

Tick. Tick. Tick . . . The bug under the floor inexorably marks the time left before our moment of white-hot illumination. But suppose the bug dies. Suppose the old man dies. And suppose the summer, which today's south wind makes good promise of, descends upon us with its blessed soporific heat. Will my fear not flee? Will the night breeze not bell the curtain and awaken desire? No. None of that. There must come the illumination. So, after supper, which is oysters tonight, and after more than my half of the bottle of Muscadet, I say to my wife, "Well, what was the old man's tale about this afternoon?"

"About a monster."

"A sea monster?" My wife nods. "With a long curving neck and sharp teeth?" I cannot keep the mockery out of my voice.

My wife knows that I'm suffering, but she knows, too, that I'm an avoider and that she must keep pushing me in the direction of the revelation we came here for. She says, "No, it was a huge squid that wrapped itself around the pier on the other side and broke the pilings when they tried to cut it loose. Finally it went away of its own accord, but it left the bay black."

I nodded slowly. "I knew it."

"Knew what?"

"That all the old man's violent raconteuring would go up in smoke. Didn't you?"

"What do you mean?"

"The giant squid was the jellied smoke of a primordial fire, a fire so hot that it boiled the sea and blued it. And you know who built that fire?" I know that my face is half demonically shrewd, half desperate. "I did. By taking away the thing she loved and trying to replace it with my paltry self." I get up from the table, knocking over the wine bottle like any histrionic drunk. "Get me to tell you about that some time." I stumble out into the night.

Five days after the fire my wife said, "You must go and talk to Peter." You see, we had recovered no photos, received no illumination from Dr. Mueller, but still could not accept the fact that all we would ever know was in our heads. So, though I dreaded the prospect, I nodded. "Yes."

No one answered my knock at the door of Elizabeth's cabin. I peeked in the window. It was afternoon, a rare bright day in early March. The light through the windows of the south-facing facade lay in luminous swatches on the bare brown floor. The cabin was deserted. And it seemed to me the sun stroked the wood more lovingly now that it was free of humans. Well, I thought, why did the sun lure us up out of the slime if it did not love us? We loved it, but it did not love us.

I went down the path to the creek, because I could not honestly report failure to my wife unless I had explored every possibility. Suppose, for instance, it was still Peter's practice to come here from some other place. And all the while I knew, of course, the danger of my returning to the creek in my present state. Here is what happened. I found that Peter was not there, but instead of relief I experienced sorrow. "Look, Peter," I said, "I will take my clothes off." I did so. And squatted down on the bank and looked at my wrinkled image riding the surface of the water, yawing downstream as though any moment it would be torn off its feeble anchorage and swept away—an image that pleased me. But I was not swept away. And predictably, my daughter appeared on the surface of the creek, between my splayed legs, beneath my drooping cullions. Naked she was, her flesh resplendently white, her bush fiery black. Some will say, I suppose, that this was a divine image of rebirth. Others will say that it was an especially poignant illumination of the male's endless dream of parturition. And still others will say that it was nothing more or less than an incestuous obscenity.

Today the images of the island begin to fade from my primary senses to a secondary level of registry. I still feel the grit of sand, still smell and taste salt, still hear the ticker and the Doppler and the finicky pipers, still meet the gull's eye with my eye. But on the primary plane stands only my wife, insisting that we push on toward illumination.

We are lying naked on the bed at dusk having taken off our swimsuits and showered away the salt, we two who have been faithful man and wife twenty years. Supperless, passionless we lie. And I am thinking, trying to get it right. "If the salt lose its savor wherein shall it be flavored?" *Flavored?*

"What do you want to tell me?" my wife says.

"I don't want to tell you, I say"

My wife sighs. We are not touching at any point, but her head is turned towards me so that I feel the little gust of her breath cross my cheek. "You need to tell me."

I roll my head vigorously. "You already know."

"No I don't. I don't know any details." The tone of her voice signifies deep deprivation. That is what I respond to.

"One time," I say, "she was reading a book in the window with her skirt down on her thighs." I swallow painfully. I look out the window. Is the gull still there listening, so that I only have to make this confession once, publish it to all persons and powers who suffered injury from my crime? I cannot tell. The sky is folded in deep gray.

"Go on."

"The window ran with rain. You were in the garden in your slicker, under her legs. And that night we made love, but I didn't make love to you." For some moments I don't say anything, and then I add, "That was once." My wife charitably leaves me a wide silence in which to go my own way. "And I lied to Peter. I told him the doctor said he and Margaret could not meet again. And he hid from her in the woods. She must've come and called and got no answer, though she would know he was there. She must've undressed by the creek and looked at the water. But instead of two, now there was only one. And so she had lost the only person in the world she ever really trusted." I pause. But my voice is not cracked. It is stronger than when I began, energized by self-hatred. "Or do you suppose there were two images?"

"What two?"

"Hers and the aging father also naked, pale, and flaccid, the animal hair on the torso more or less intact, but the lower legs scraped bare by years of wearing pants. And the face crossed with goatish lust. Don't you think so?"

"Perhaps. And a third image too."

From the creek I went to Quilty's cabin. This was a Saturday afternoon so I assumed he would be at the gallery. Perhaps I would find Peter alone. But the opposite was the case. Quilty answered the door. Peter was not there. "Come on in," said Quilty in a voice surprisingly full of feeling. We had not seen each other since the fire. He sat me down in an old rocker that creaked, but felt safe. "Rest."

I did rest. I laid my head back and shut my eyes, relieved not to have to look at the wacky posters. I said, "We're going to an island, way down in the Gulf of Mexico."

"That's good. Elizabeth, my ex, has gone down that way with a dude from Louisiana. It'll be a good place for you, warm and friendly."

"We're not going in order to forget," I said, suddenly aware that I was very drowsy, had lost track of my mission. "Where's Peter? Did he go with his mother?"

"No, he's here, out in the woods somewhere."

"I want to talk to him," I said. I thought Quilty might give me a preview of Peter's condition, but he didn't. I could've asked directly, of course, how he had taken Margaret's death, but instead I said, "How's your work going, the big broadside?"

"I can't do it."

"Why not?"

"It would be too sad. The new age that didn't come, in spite of all that burned themselves up trying to make it come." Should that have made me angry? Was he analogizing my Margaret to the acid heads and speed freaks that burned themselves out in the sixties? No. I don't think so. He went on. "It's not good to do sad art. You should do beauty art or apocalypse art, but depression art is bad."

"You'd better tell some of your current practitioners," I said.

"In the gallery I don't hang depression art." I didn't say anything to that. A long silence followed, broken at last by Quilty, who spoke in a hushed incredulous voice. "How can you just sit there with your eyes closed and rock, man?"

"Why not?"

"I mean when this thing we've been talking about has come down on you in one big blaze. I even saw it in the sky that night, but I didn't know what it was."

"You know now?"

"I know, but I can't say it."

I opened my eyes and shook my head. "It wasn't any of this apocalyptic bullshit, Quilty. Any of this star-wafer world-body acid dream bullshit. It was a fire, with my daughter in the middle of it."

"Third image?" I say to my wife, exhausted by self-flagellation. "What is the third image?"

"The third image is me," she says.

"You? You were never at the creek," I say, proprietary, petulant.

"Yes, but I loved her too much."

I don't want to hear this. I am the grand villain, impresario of fire. The role of my wife (though I have alleged that her very virtue was contributory to the tragedy) is merely to press us toward illumination here on the island. But now, if she is the third image, also a deep sinner, then everything will be agonizingly complex. I don't want to hear it. But I can't stop her.

"I memorized every detail of her pink little body and every change as it started to go lean and beautiful."

I Pat my wife's hands. "You don't have to confess this. There's nothing the matter with it."

She doesn't seem to hear me. "When she was a child it could be excused as overfondness maybe—I mean holding her in my lap too long, combing her hair too long, going in at night too many times to see if she was all right."

Suddenly I remember a curious habit my wife had when Margaret was small. Whenever we made love, she would get up out of bed afterwards, put on her robe, brush her hair, and go into Margaret's room, instead of lolling with me under the warm covers. Nevertheless, I say, "There's nothing wrong with that."

"Yes," she says, "but when she got older I still wanted to touch her. But I couldn't so I just looked at her and looked at her." My wife turns more sharply in my direction. It is almost dark, but we can still see each other's eyes. "Do you think," she says, "it's possible to project yourself into somebody else?"

"In dreams or visions maybe," I say.

"So I dreamed myself into her," says my wife, picking up my suggestion immediately, pressing rapidly on toward the expression of this strange experience. "Often. And hid there inside her, waiting to feel what she felt." My wife does not go on.

"Well," I say, impatient but also fearful, "did you?"

"Yes," says my wife, beginning to weep softly.

"What was it?"

My wife is sobbing now and cannot answer.

I dozed a long while in Quilty's rocker. The images of fire had faded from my mind and I had fallen into a dreamless sleep. When I awoke, Peter was sitting in a chair at the oak table, looking at me. I didn't know how long he had been there, but I knew that considerable time had passed, for the shaft of sunlight through the window was much more acute, more golden. But how did I appear to him just then? As something still threatening even in my somnolence? Apparently, for he eyed me with the wariness of a forest creature.

"I went to the creek," I said, "and took my clothes off, but nobody came."

Quilty, who was sitting slightly behind and to the left of Peter, gave me a strange look. The aim of my statement was to establish contact with Peter immediately, cut back through the adult world of clothes and cabin to the elemental concerns we had spoken of by the creek. Maybe I shouldn't have said it in front of Quilty. But I had no choice. He was simply there, immovably there, Peter's father, an irritating but very human misfortune—head muddled by the impossible visions of the sixties, a pseudo-artist, generous, hospitable, incapable of domestic responsibility. And yet he still had his child. Well, not really, but his child still lived, and that was more than I could say. Nevertheless I didn't envy him, because maybe it was better to lose a child in a single searing blaze than to lose one piecemeal. I said, "Anything we have to say to each other your father can hear." I paused a moment for that to settle amongst us.

"Why do you think she burned herself up?" Peter said nothing. I went on. "I'm asking for myself but I'm also asking for Margaret's mother. She cries a lot and can't sleep. Only part of it is because she lost Margaret. The other part is because she doesn't understand." Something painful crossed Peter's face. Maybe it was the contrast between Margaret's mother and his own mother, who had just dumped him and gone south with her boyfriend. "Would you ever think of burning yourself up?"

He shook his head decisively.

"What would you think of?"

"Going into the creek maybe."

"Why would you think of that?"

He shrugged—not evasively, but to show that he found words difficult. "School and things. What we talked about."

I nodded. "Yes, but I don't think Margaret worried that much about school. I don't think she sweated or smoked." Quilty's eyes registered surprise. I thought, if nothing else comes of this visit, maybe at least he will understand his child better. I pressed on. "So what worried Margaret?"

Peter looked down at the yellowed fingers of his right hand. "She worried about everything, about me and other kids."

"Go on," I said, but he remained silent. "Go on, Peter," I urged gently. "You were going to say something."

"She worried about what was happening to the woods and the creek and the animals." He looked pained, abashed, so I nodded that I understood. I didn't trust my voice because my mind was torn by warring emotions. On the one hand I was deeply moved by my dead daughter's universal sympathy. On the other, a surge of mordant cynicism filled me with self-reproach—that I had allowed a child to go out that tender and unprotected into this butcher's world. Suddenly Peter spoke again, his voice rising. "I did what you told me. When she came, I hid in the woods." That was as far as he could go. A violent hitch in his chest stopped him. He began to sob.

The tears ran down from my eyes, too, but oddly my voice was restored. "Can you ever forgive me, Peter? I have to tell you that I lied. The doctor didn't tell me that Margaret shouldn't see you. I made that up."

Peter had bent his head down, but now he looked up again. Never have I seen a child's eyes so full of pity.

"What did you feel there inside Margaret?" I say, harshly, insistently. My wife's weeping has begun to harrow me. There has been too much weeping.

"Naked!" she cries out, her voice surprisingly strong. "And not just naked to the skin, not just naked to the bones but naked to the very core of feeling." As in the days when we first came here to the island my wife again wishes to flay me with her nails. I can feel it quite clearly, as though the very air between us were scarified. So the vision of my own ritual violence is awakened too. I would like to crouch over her and, as if in the subaqueous medium of a dream, slowly pound her blue with my fists.

"You will never know such nakedness," my wife says, "not even if you stripped and crouched by all the creeks in the world. Not if you looked up and saw a thousand eyes looking in at every window. Not if a camera followed you everywhere you went and took pictures of you whatever you did and printed them in newspapers and spread them all over the world."

If I had said that, it would have been mere extravagance, but in my wife's mouth it is piercing. The roots of my tongue are dry and twisted. I croak when I speak. "What did it feel like?"

"Beyond feelings." My wife pauses. Something seems to peer up over the edge of her mind. "Some crazy woman has written a book about a child that got burned horribly and yet lived. But the skin couldn't repair itself and there wasn't enough left for transplants, so the child became a living wound."

The air around us is drawn painfully. I say, "I will never read that book." Nevertheless, the image of fire rises up in my mind again—the white-hot A with a crimson corona hovering just above. And once again black smoke billows into the inverted sea of night and extinguishes the stars. Suddenly I reach out and grasp my wife by the wrist. "But the opposite of pure nakedness is not loathsome guilt."

"What is it then?"

"It's not guilt." I squeeze her wrist tighter. "We're not guilty."

"Yes. I agree," says my wife, obviously surprised, "but then why did we think of our ugly bodies by the creek?"

"I don't know," I say. "Maybe because guilt is better than nothing. Because it's too hard to admit that even love can't hold on to its objects—if love can't hold on, what can? So we conceived of guilt, to explain it."

There is a long silence. Then my wife says, "Can't you tell me what the opposite of pure nakedness is?"

"No." I get up from the bed. I grope and find my wife's hand again and help her up. The ticker under the floor is quiet. I lead my wife out of the cabin onto the sand, which is still very warm. In the absence of moon the stars are bright. From behind the cabin, in the dune grass, the crickets and other insects make a happy din that rises easily over the slow slosh of the sea. And once, twice before we reach the sea's edge the Doppler passes, zinging in, thrumming off, on his amazing orbit. My wife says, "You're going to take me skinny-dipping." What is that in her voice? An improbable note of girlishness?

Does this sound irresponsible? Having gotten to the threshold, did we step back, childish and afraid? I don't think so. There on the bed in the cabin we had gone as far as we could go. Neither my wife's quiet frankness nor my rhetorical flourishes could take us any further. What human, except maybe a great mystic, could go further? "Yes," I say, "I'm taking you skinny-dipping. And when we get back to the cabin, the gull will not be spying on us. And tomorrow the pipers will eat out of our hands. The old man will tell us the story of the island's most famous lovers, or else we won't listen to him. And the great summer sun will rise in the East."

But my wife is no longer listening. She is already thigh-deep in the sea and now flings her arms out to dive forward. I must hurry after her.

THE UNCLE

How much revolver *would* you need to kill a man? The question, according to the uncle, a former agent, had been studied, with insignificant results. A blighter dark against a window at night could, excepting sudden illumination by torch or thunderbolt, hardly be killed at all, so porous with shadow was he.

The boy sat on a stool at the uncle's feet. Sometimes he made pictures in his mind of the alleys and corridors of moon, of the flash and roar of midnight chase. Sometimes he merely let the words ring and settle, one by one, knowing without fear that he would not lose them, that at school or on the edge of sleep they would float up, dislodged from the deep anchorages of his brain. His mind, he knew, was miles deep, despite the fact that his father, smiling a mild reproof, still could join thumbs and middle fingers in a ring around his head. "Are you paying attention at school, boy? Your cranium is not expanding at a very rapid rate."

"I'm paying attention."

Attention, according to the uncle, was inherently intermittent, the moon behind a sky of scudding clouds. The art that the master criminals knew so well was how to proceed along attention's interstices, as RikkiTikkiTavi struck in the cobra's eye-blink. Bullets were useless with such.

"Have you told him about Nina Kristeva?" said the father.

No, for the boy's ears had not heard, eyes seen enough yet to ready him for Kristeva. They could arrive at her only by proceeding first along the less tortuous paths laid by such as Ned Brinkin, the Morpheus Man, Gunnar the Gunner, and Pio Aguello.

At each sitting a certain time was allowed, though the boy could not have told just how many minutes, before the mother came and said invariably, "You have worried Uncle 'Lando long enough. He needs to get to his work."

No, said the uncle, the attendance of the boy on his maunderings helped prime the pumps of memory. But the mother's declaration was fell. So the boy would slip into his baby sister's room and poke her in the belly, which at first made her laugh and then, with unsmiling mechanical repetition, whimper, upon which he left. She was a null anyway, but he understood, with dread, how she was sucking her way into the world, engorging huge portions of attention and affection.

The uncle was writing a memoir at his great secretary, which, much higher than the boy's head, sloped down like a portly gentleman's vest, and opened out into a miraculous triptych. From the central panel a green felt writing surface lowered like a drawbridge over the deep tarn of the uncle's adventures. On either side of the writing surface were rows and rows of cubbyholes, each filled with a green-faced box that was labeled and furnished, for easy removal, with a small brass ring in the mouth of a miniature lion. The labels were various: Ned Brinkin, Law, Cadet, Morpheus Man, Nina Kristeva, etc. Some were as yet unlabeled. One hundred in all, these were five wide and ten high in each of the two massive doors.

The question was how to proceed, how to arrange the boxes, which the uncle changed in some small respect virtually daily. "Why don't you just go from start to finish, Uncle 'Lando?" the mother suggested.

A false analogy based on gestation, parturition, and maturation, my dear girl, the uncle said, patting the mother's hand if she was near enough, and often issuing compensatory flatteries to take off the edge of his contradiction, especially if it was evening and he was taking his nip of brandy: eyes like doves, a lily of the valley, a singing rill, a smile like a pomegranate or a honeycomb, spikenard and saffron, sugar cane and cinnamon, a tower of ivory, a gazelle.

"Uncle 'Lando, if I didn't have a husband and these two children, you would turn my head."

How would he write it, then? Perhaps he would shackle it like a snake with its tale in its mouth. This was Ned Brinkin's favorite ploy—to raise an indomitable ring of dust until even the rank kudzu was so densely powdered that it flagged and gave back no hint of moon, its tree-high festoons gray and slack-bellied as old cobwebs. But you could not throw a net of local constabulary over old Ned, for his circumference, within the tight confines of his game, was diabolically variable. Otherwise, it would have been possible to practice a crude cartography, place a finger tip just so, issue orders and leave the locale to elevate itself from its own cowering. But no, he, Orlando, himself had to determine where at some precise nick of the clock in that maelstrom of pulverized earth and persiflage of artfully placed phone calls the mobile villain paused for a breath. Old Ned was a case—altogether different, of course, from the innocent tigerish plunges of Gunnar, the bee-dance of diminutive Pio, the filigree and lattices of the Morpheus Man, or the extraordinary inventiveness of Kristeva's triangulation. That, boy, was what made it all worthwhile. Oh, in Kristeva's case he received special commendation for protecting the secrets of the state, but even that paled in the agony and splendor of the process.

"What secrets of the state?" the boy wanted to know, but his mother came and shooed him away. Well, the state was more or less a rectangle turned long ways up, with a funny-looking tip-toe by the gulf. The flower was the goldenrod and the bird the flicker. The secrets, then, must be something under the ground. Even the picture of the all-black legislature the Yankees put in after the war was still on a wall of the state house, his father said. So it was nothing in time past. "What are the secrets of the state?" he asked his mother, who was holding his baby sister's heels up, powdering her buttocks, and joining her in an obscene rictus of sensuality.

"If I knew, they wouldn't be secrets, would they?"

"Do you think Uncle 'Lando knew?"

"No, he didn't have to know to protect them."

"Where do they keep them?"

"In their heads and on papers."

"That's what I'm going to be when I grow up.

"What?"

"One of the ones who keeps the secrets of the state."

"Why on earth would you want to do that?"

"Because my mind is miles deep."

"How many miles?"

"I don't know. All the stuff I have ever heard or seen is piled up down there, but it's hardly covered the bottom yet."

"Do you think you can rummage around down there and find any of the things the teacher tells you?"

"I can try."

"Please do."

The house to which the uncle had come to pass his seniority with access to companionship and creature comforts sat on a hillside in the motley shade of two big brindled sycamores. The retired agent was quartered on the sun porch, which the father had converted with paneling, glass, and carpeting into a handsome all-weather room. "He will have both light and shade," said the father philosophically, "a nice place to be while things are slipping away from you."

"Nothing is slipping away from him. It's all coming back," said the boy.

In the case of Kristeva, said the uncle, no one had any idea who it was. All they knew was that it was a case of triangulation. You needed two others and the exact arcs of their defection to identify the third, the master spy. But in the case of Old Ned Brinkin, it was not identity, but locus that was in question. Oh, they got him all right. It was not miscalculation on Brinkin's part or genius on the uncle's. It was ennui. It's the freedom they can't stand, boy.

"Why would he want to go to jail?"

The bars and filial strips show that he is society's son again. You look confounded, boy. Take those marbles out of your pocket and toss them in the air. Again. Now, granted that on a thicker carpet, they would not bound and scamper so wantonly, still you would not know how they would land, would you?

The boy shook his head. "No, but the reason the rug isn't thick is because you don't pick your feet up when you walk."

How much fun, the uncle wanted to know, would it be to toss the marbles up all day. None, of course. You see it, then, boy. It's the dispossession and the randomness of criminal freedom they come to hate. But this was not so in Kristeva's case, for her function as receiver and ultimate relayer of the secrets required her continual presence in a certain place. Great God, boy, that such a tour d'ivoire, drenched in moonlight, the alps to her pinnacle nothing but the low hummocks of common clay, the whole world in fact nothing but a grammar school child's Egypt of flour paste—a watercolor Nile, the pyramids cheap studs awled from an old dog's collar, that such a one should raise herself against the law and stretch man on the rack of duty and desire.

The boy's sister kicked her feet in the air and gooed. A rattle hung from a band of elastic strung over her crib and made its ancient beady noise. The pink flesh puffed sweetly on her arms and legs, and the little belly bounced as she kicked. The boy stuck his finger against her palm and she clamped down on it automatically but paid no attention to him, her eyes fastened on the translucent rattle. In this stage, said the uncle, shuffling cribside, all the world is but an ex-tension of her senses, the great meadows that man has named, rended, analyzed, still in her eye as integral as the dots and dabs of a Seurat in yours and mine.

In his fantasies and in his dreams, the great subterranean shelves of the boy's mind started into a bizarre animation of Woman. The perfume of cinna-mon talc scented the air. Seaweed yearned upward through watery showers of light. A dove oared with stately strokes along the undulant surface, a lily in its beak. Deer came down in the dark to nibble dusty kudzu. Bees swarmed in honeysuckle. But overshadowing all towered a white basilisk tippeted by moon-light that guttered and spilled down from the cloud-piercing pinnacle. And all the while there beat a strange susurrus, melodious and rhythmic. The boy half expected to see the basilisk soften and sway into dance. It made him dizzy. He reached for solider stuff. "What were the secrets of state you saved from Kristeva, Uncle 'Lando?"

The uncle was working at his secretary, the monstrous doors swung back, the drawbridge down, and several of the lion-head cubby boxes pulled forward. He was scribing notes on thick cards and depositing them variously into Commendation, Mulier, Pio, Kristeva, etc. There were now three boxes marked Kristeva. The uncle turned his swivel chair and presented the boy a smiling face. He swayed and moved his arms out and up in the fashion of a Bali dancer. What animal am I, boy, and do not answer homo sapiens, for I mean figuratively. "A badger." No, a badger would scutter on his belly and hiss, whereas I am upright and all happily abuzz.

"A bee. And your desk is your honeycomb."

Smart lad. And the memoir was not a story, though his niece, the mother, persisted in thinking it so. It was a testament, a cornucopia, a full gra-nary, a honeycomb, against the lean years. To some the fat comes in dreams, to others in memory—in either case all unbidden and unearned, a blessing and a burden. It must be stored for the coming generations. Here, for instance, is Gunnar. The uncle fished out of a cubby a pack of index cards and riffled them like a gambler. If the globe had been flat, they never would have nabbed him.

London, Paris, Istanbul, Johannesburg, Sierra Leone, Karachi, Göteborg, New York—Euclid himself could not have described the polygons his crossings made. But earth's round surface at length turned him back on himself. They found him in an old farm loft in Massachusetts, once a Shaker colony. He was asleep on his side, his knees curled up, his head on his hands, like a dreamer in a picture book. Against the moonlit wall leaned the rifle, which, had they not stolen into his sleep, would have wreaked havoc on the posse.

"Well," said the father, "who have you done so far?"

"Old Ned and Gunnar," said the boy.

"Then there's only little Pio and the Morpheus Man before you get to Kristeva." The father ran his hand rapidly through the boy's hair. "Think of that."

But the uncle held out a wavering hand toward the father and in a quavering voice declared that he wasn't sure if he could tell the story of Kristeva again.

"Well," said the father softly, seeing that his enthusiastic anticipation had misfired, "you don't have to tell it again. We can all read it in your memoirs."

"No," said the boy. "He has to tell it because what if he never writes the memoirs?"

The mother called him away and looked at him with a mixture of disappointment and surprise. "You're a bright boy. Can't you tell that old people don't like to be bossed and told that their time may run out?"

"Well, if he would just go ahead and tell about the state secrets. Everybody knows the story but me."

"That's right, and if you get sassy with Uncle 'Lando again, you won't ever hear it."

"You better not take me away from him, because I'm the only one that will sit and listen to him."

"Uppity! Mmm!" The mother widened her eyes. "If you don't straighten out, one of Uncle 'Lando's agents will come and put you in the penitentiary in a striped suit with a ball and chain around your ankle and a bloodhound that smells you night and day in case you try to escape."

The boy couldn't stand to leave his mother on a cross note, so he said, "What's a Shaker?"

"You mean those old-timey religious fanatics?"

"I guess so."

"Then it was a group that worked all day with tools and at night they would get together and sing and shake, which kept them so busy that they never had any children."

"I declare," said the boy, imitating his mother. "Did they just forget?"

"Go on, now. I'm busy."

The father and the uncle stood by the crib admiring the baby, who was kicking, widening her eyes, smiling, and gooing. "Now, what in the hell do you suppose she thinks she's doing?" said the father.

The uncle spoke of the famous inverted pyramid. Every individual's whole person rested on the narrow fulcrum of his infancy. If the first stones were sound, then the great edifices of soul, psyche, and body withstood all weathers. But if the stones were loose or shaley, then it was a house built on sand.

"I don't think we have to worry about this one, do you, Uncle 'Lando? I think she's going to be as sound and sunny as her mother." The uncle nodded agreement.

"What kind of infancy did I have?" the boy asked his mother.

"Normal. Normal in every way."

But the boy saw that his person was not a pyramid, though the basilisk still towered up in his mind whenever he thought of Kristeva. His person, as far as he could tell, was a beehive of rummage. "My name is Joannie," wrote the girl in the next desk at school, but he couldn't get his letters to march along the line. They curled up toward the top of the page and then he filled in all the a's, e's, and o's, because he didn't like the blank holes. So when the teacher laid his work out on his desk for parents night, it looked like waves with little black balls tumbling under the crests. Everybody was to leave a note. His said,

And he wondered if his baby sister was really making a pyramid. She seemed to him nothing but dots, the kind of dots they made the numbers out of at school to see if you were color blind. Earl couldn't see the yellow-green 7, and nothing could ever be done for him; but he didn't care, he said, because it wasn't the kind of 7 they ever used. The baby's person was just dots. Uncle 'Lando had said so himself.

Was Uncle 'Lando a pyramid? The secretary was like a piece of one that unfolded. It didn't have mummies, but it had cubbies that were like the tombs in New Orleans. They had to bury above ground there, Uncle 'Lando said, all stacked up, or the Mississippi River seeped into the coffins. Maybe some day Uncle 'Lando would stop shuffling and just stand there like a pyramid, like the secretary. But the boy didn't think so. He got the idea that Kristeva was the only one who stood forever as a tower, that everybody else was laid low and crumbled. It wouldn't happen to him, though, because he was just a bunch of rummage. If you didn't build up, you didn't have to fall down. Let the baby build up into a pyramid, if she didn't have the gumption not to. He was going to go through on his belly hissing like a badger. Well, maybe even Kristeva, the moonlight basilisk, would eventually fall down, but he would survive.

Ah, the Morpheus Man. The uncle tasted his lips as he did when he sipped brandy. In olden times they called him the Shape Shifter. You thought you abided on a solid globe, stepping surely through the mild circumambient air in the predictable light of sun and moon. You thought your flesh was safely sealed and your senses tenacious graspers of the Outthere. And then you met the Morpheus Man, the master of disguise and subterfuge. All the world became a fatally perforated hall of mirrors. At the Palace in Versailles the Morpheus Man was a footman in the livery of the Sun King, and then a pale sea creature spitting ocean into a huge scallop shell, and then a sculptured bush, and then its afternoon shadow, and then nothing at all, until the whole cadre of agents was frozen in the garden looking into each others' eyes, a polygon of narcissi.

"How could you ever catch him?"

You tell me, boy. How could you net a thing that disassembled and reconstructed itself at will? How could you shoot a thing already full of holes? How could you manacle wrists as malleable as beeswax?

"What had he done wrong?"

Murder by misperception. Without ever actually touching any victim, much less driving a knife or firing a shot, and even without setting a trap, he dispatched a half dozen, including two of my best agents. With what, precisely? Precipices, pits, weirs, the famous maelstrom, inter alia. Well, the thing to do was get him into a place as solid as he was porous. Rome, Paris, New York, Buenos Aires, London. Which do you think, boy?

"London?"

London it was. Oh, London has its tubes, its mews, its quaint closes, its labyrinthine parks and fogs, but she is solid, boy, quintessentially solid. After the fire, they laid stones—stone streets, stone buildings, stone arches, and cornered it sharp. If only we could lure the Morpheus Man to London. The uncle's eyes brightened moistly with memory. Yes, and he was game, God bless him. All of them were, eventually. Keeping to their own ground, they might have triumphed indefinitely, but that would have been mere repetition, and repetition is a kind of death. Down deep in all of us, boy, there's a base beat that simply wants to go on and on. But against that is a little impish fellow. Do you hear him make his irregular ping? Little Pio it was that taught me this.

"What about the Morpheus Man? Where did you catch him?"

In the Banqueting Hall. He was a buxom server. He was a boar with an apple in his mouth. He was the rum flame wavering from your Lord Mayor's half-acre pudding. But all to no avail. It was not only the walls. It was the pink flesh, boy, of all those Rubens. You cannot slip into a Rubens. Even the shadows in the crux of the arm and the dimple of the knee are burnished against entry. We triced him, but knowing that would not suffice, we put him in a locked sedan and carried him down the London streets like an infamous flame and ringed the sedan, too, with three concentric circles of agents. And even at that, we held our breath when we unlocked the sedan in Scotland Yard.

Now all this while, autumn yellowed the sycamores and hung them with hard seed balls. The wind got down into the grass and tousled it. The ants ran underground. The large panes the father had installed on the screen porch waffled and gave back a peculiar curled light. "Maybe he doesn't want to tell any more stories for a while," the mother said, scooping into the baby's mouth a little spoon of dun-colored mush. The boy couldn't stand to watch the stuff bubble at his sister's lips. "You'll just have to be patient."

"Okay, but when he doesn't talk, he just piddles with the boxes, moving them all around and changing the labels and the cards."

"He has to do that to figure out how to write his memoirs."

"He's never going to write anything down but the cards."

The mother looked at him sharply. "What did I tell you about that?" The baby made a dismissive flailing of her arms. "Booo! Fooo!"

The boy went to watch the uncle shuffle the cubbies. The next day, the father came in and sat down. The uncle's white hair was mussed, and his hands strayed pitifully among the green boxes. He scarcely acknowledged his visitors. The father said, "I don't know about you, Uncle 'Lando, but November gives me the willies."

Well, said the uncle, turning an unresolved eye in the father's direction, his had not been a seasonal calling, nor was he going to submit now in retirement to autumnal fits and spleen, though, God knew, it was not a propitious time to tell of Kristeva.

"No, indeed," said the father, "but what about little Pio? Do you have all your cards on him together?"

The uncle pulled out the box marked *Aguello* and looked inside. Yes, there was something there. He tried to hide his surprised satisfaction and to appear casual as he shuffled through the cards. Little, said the uncle, was an unfortunate epithet, an all too apparent attempt on the part of the agents to domesticate one of the most daring criminals of all time.

"What did he do wrong?" said the boy.

Some would say nothing, boy. The uncle smiled a crooked smile. Let us say he breached several borders. The great river where once the waters laved Mexican soil on the upper as well as on the nether lip and the vaulted walls between certain hoards of verdant presidential portraits and the hands of Yaquis, distributors to the innumerable destitute of Chihuahua. Do you take my meaning, boy?

"You mean money?"

But the most profound border he breached, bright lad, was the one between reality and myth. You cannot map that ocean, boy. That's why the old cartographers dotted the blue expanses with mermaids, sea monsters, and the like. Nor could you anchor in a trench where the fishes were all mouth and glowing eye, so far below the flukes that even the rattle of chain in the hawser pipe came to them like the clutter of distant pebbles. So they chased him back and forth over the Rio. And the officialdom waggled its mustachios. "Si, senores, ha pasado por aqui hace pocos momentos. Buena suerte." Yes, they were always only moments behind, but that was inevitable, because all Pio's traffic was undulation. You can catch water in a basin, boy, but you can't catch a wave. So they needed more than luck. They might have employed a bloodhound, but he would have taken them to the Gulf of Mexico, for the chemistries of ocean and blood are very similar. Did you know that, boy?

"You mean, he killed a lot of people?"

That would be pure calumny. The only thing Pio spilled was money. It sprang up in the desert behind him like flowers. And they followed, as drones do the dance of the discoverer, sipping the dew from the little tuckets of honeysuckle; for no matter what inn or tavern they entered, his largesse had preceded them; nor food nor lodging could be paid for by the agents. Paradoxically, they grew gaunt, their cheeks hollow, their eyes dark-rimmed, until one night, crossing over in a skiff with a quiet electric motor, they found themselves on the most ancient of rivers, the Nile. And, their boat became the sad little bark into which keening Isis scooped from crocodiles' jaws the parts of her poor dismembered brother. And there above us... (The uncle lifted his hand and pointed above his head. His voice quavered.)...we saw a wavering pyramid that scribed our fate on the midnight sky, but who could untangle that strange calligraphy, more dazzling than the scripts of Hejaz.

The November wind buffeted the porch panes, flashing an intermittent image of the uncle, his wintry mane against the green front and petite brass lions of the secretary. The father and the boy watched his face contract painfully. Kristeva, he called. You were there even then, weren't you? Oh God, that such a tower of beauty should raise herself against the law!

"How did he say they caught Pio the last time he told it?" the boy wanted to know. The uncle had eaten some milk toast, taken a little brandy, and submitted to the mother's wish that he go to bed early. She had kissed him on the forehead and he had lifted his hand to her cheek. She was his lovely four-winged angel who would winnow out the bad dreams from the good.

"Well." The father stroked his chin. "As I recall, they used a woman. Cherchez la femme."

They were at the supper table. The baby was slapping into the highchair board some goo she had dribbled from her mouth. The boy couldn't look at it. "What do you mean, they used a woman?"

"As bait. Little Pio was an amorous sort, it turned out."

The mother looked sharply at the father. "I don't think you have it right, but it doesn't matter, because we're not going to have Uncle 'Lando tell any more stories. It's wearing him down."

"Goo! Foo!"

"The baby is smiling at you. Can't you smile back to your own little sister?"

The boy decided to have a dream. He was a hunter who had gone into the forest before daybreak with his rifle on his shoulder. It was late fall, and the cold air tumbling down the mountain killed his odor in the deer's nose. The day before, he had practiced with his rifle, shooting black holes in the a's, e's, and o's of Joannie and several other words. He never missed. He checked his compass and set his course due north, toward the pool in the river where the deer drank. He passed from a brindled dawn of ash and alder onto a narrow meadow of dry golden rod where lately the bees had feasted. The last wisps of fog were taking leave of the pool, its surface disturbed only now and then by a quick-sliding little whirligig. He took station behind a large stone. Just before the deer came, he noticed for the first time the broken stakes of the weir the Indians had built many years before in the shoaling water near the mouth of the pool. She was preceded by a cinnamon musk. So he knew it was her even before he saw the horns like basilisks tipped with the goldenpink light of the early sun. He aimed and fired. Down crashed the deer into the pool, and the water went all red. "Oh. Kristeva, why did you raise your beautiful horns against the law!"

"My Lord," said the mother, swinging open his bedroom door. "What kind of nightmare are *you* having?"

"Who else is having one?"

"Uncle 'Lando was just now thrashing and shouting in his sleep about that Kristeva woman."

"He's quiet now," said the father, coming up behind the mother. "But the baby's awake."

"Some night." The mother went to see to the baby.

"What's the matter with you, boy?"

"Nothing. I was just having a dream."

The mother persuaded the uncle to take a day off from his labors. A mid-week sabbath, the uncle said, bending over the crib and offering the baby a finger to grasp. But she would know nothing of weeks.

"What about days?" the boy said.

Nor days. She sees only the totality of things. The child is the father of the man. In her there is no east or west, no seasons or years or epochs or eons.

"I'll bet she knows the difference between night and day."

If not now, soon. The uncle sighed.

The next afternoon, when the boy went to see the uncle on the sun porch, he beheld a terrible sight. All the boxes of the secretary were pulled out like so many green tongues and all were empty, the cards in a heap on the floor and also the little labels, torn from their slots below the lions' mouths. The uncle gave the boy a look of desperate wisdom. Do not start and look afraid, boy. Did you not listen carefully to the words spoken over your infant sister's crib? This follows hard upon.

"Are you going to write your memoirs like rummage?"

Disingenuous question! Obviously there was to be no memoir. For to commit to black and white, serialize in days and nights the great cornucopia of memory was a desecration. God forbid that he should be caught in the trap of a passion for analysis. Hadn't Little Pio, wafting on the waves of the ancient river, taught him better? It was never in these cards, boy. That was my illusion. It was only here. He tapped his head beneath his gray hair. And as soon as I have finished the telling of Kristeva, then where will it be, boy? Slowly, the boy lifted his hand and tapped his own head. And after that, where will it be, boy?

"I don't know. Where?"

The uncle tapped a head that was not entirely his own. In your boy's.

"What if there isn't any?"

The uncle swallowed. Then it will be where it has always been. Are you ready for the story of Kristeva?

The boy looked back to make sure that his mother wasn't coming. "Yes."

The uncle placed his fingertips together to steady each set, one against the other, and still his old hands quaked fearfully. You do not go in search of an absolute, boy. Even we understood that, mere detectives though we were, jaded by greed and romance, by the endless spectacle of ennui and self-defeat. The question was, had the inventions of such as Pio and the Morpheus Man prepared us for this consummation? The arrangement, we knew, was a triptych, but who were the personages? Meanwhile, the secrets of the state were violated, poised perhaps within the grasp of nefarious hands. At length a photograph was delivered—a face longer than an El Greco, spade-bearded, fell as a truncheon, the first of the triptych.

He would be in the capital, of course, that irradiant and intentional city, his angularity piercing our New World innocence. But the city was full of such. Nevertheless, we found him, an ersatz eccentric of the park, where he winded a ram's horn, calling all within hearing to a great inauguration. We rejoiced, but prematurely, for the first did not lead immediately to the second. The spade-beard pursued his mad routines, made no phone calls, dropped no messages, flashed nothing from a mirror, but remained benignly encapsulated in his ancient prophecies. A cul-de-sac? No, it must be, sometime, somehow, that he communicated to the next. How do you suppose, boy?

"He sent out messages on a homing pigeon."

The uncle bent over his tented fingers and looked glowingly into the boy's eyes. Boy, two things are required for greatness in an agent: the minor, powers of ratiocination; the major, intuition. It this latter, I judge you to have extraordinary promise. The uncle leaned back. The pigeons, however, were not homing pigeons. They were ordinary park pigeons, and they did not carry the messages but left them. Where the spade-beard strewed popcorn like a careless sower, there remained always two or three uneaten, pecked up and dropped again. Along came a mountain of a jolly man, wheezing and tutting in the green shade and on the spiked tip of his ebony cane gathered up the ersatz popcorn, wadded papers. Whereupon this rolling alp slowly returned to a pair of huge bronze doors that opened and closed behind him like an encapsulation of sunrise and sunset, his shiny bald pate catching briefly the diurnal sheen. And we rejoiced, again prematurely, for the mountain had only appeared to come to Mohammed. Day in and day out, punctuated with much dormancy and much ingestion of food, drink, and message, the alp passed through the golden gate, took its reflection, graced the park, and returned. Oh, weary round. We had the mind and the body, boy, but not the soul. The uncle's little tent of fingers collapsed. Oh, that such a tour d'ivoire should raise its resplendent pinnacle in the night of evil.

"So you had to figure out how the alp got the spade-beard's messages to the tower."

Tara! Roland to the dark tower came. How do you think, boy?

"At night, in an Egyptian boat."

The uncle narrowed his eyes. Such a dark ferry would indeed have been appropriate. But in fact, the messages were delivered cartographically by shrewd, almost imperceptible variance. Do you take my meaning, boy?

"The way he walked back and forth through the park?"

Aye, but from what skyey vantage, boy, must the eye see that registered those minor sinuosities?

"From an obelisk or a tower."

But suppose there was no such to be seen?

"Maybe they put something in space or on the moon."

"Goo! Foo!" The boy turned to see the mother standing in the doorway with the baby in her arms. The baby was straining out and down toward the glittering heap of cards on the carpet. A globule of spittle, hanging from her nether lip, caught the brindled light that passed from sun through sycamore and porch pane. "It's time," said the mother with ominous finality, eyeing the heap of cards. But the uncle spoke. My dear, give us just five minutes and we shall be done with these plaguey narratives of crime. I promise. The wheel has come full circle.

The mother relented after a hesitation during which she seemed to contemplate speaking of the cards and then to think better of it. "All right, Uncle 'Lando, five more minutes, and then send him on to me in the kitchen. I've got chores for him."

Yes, my dear. The uncle stared after her. That one is a lily of the valley, boy, a doe in a field of saffron and spices, the dove that unfurls the rainbow. The uncle snapped his eyes back. But this other one's pinnacle poisoned the very sky and made it jaundiced at cherry blossom time.

"How did she see how the fat man walked?"

Took a lesson from King Tut and his legions. Fire could not be taken into the inner sanctum of the pyramid, for it would burn away the oxygen. So the sun's rays must be caught in a huge mirror at the desert's marge and by an intricate series of prisms shot down the slant corridors and into the burial chamber where the king's painter limned on the wall Thoth the bird god. And every few minutes the mirror and the prisms had to be adjusted to the course of the sun. Imagine it, boy!

The image of the rolling alp's burnished pate passed, by a series of tiny tree-mounted reflectors and prisms, to a penthouse, where we found a green awning, pots of impatiens showing their little faces to the sun, white wrought-iron chairs, table, chaise lounge, a beach towel imprinted with a bronze smiling zodiac, for it was May now and unseasonably warm. We were received like long awaited guests, our warrant treasured as though it were the embossed card of a marquis. The leader, Orlando Gillett, armed, stiff in his gray suit, abashed, accepted her hand and her congratulations. Oh ermine, oh velveteen evil! To have held in one's eyes, by injunctions of extraordinary vigilance, that tower of ivory flesh and by command not to have blinked. To have been touched, to have held fast and still to have lost her. All surged forward, too late. Out upon the unbuoyant air she swam, the petite impatiens nodding in the sad little gust of her departure, her black hair streaming up like seaweed in the oblique currents. And faint Orlando almost followed, but the other agents held him back.

After some moments, during which the uncle looked with red-rimmed eyes down into what appeared a fathomless space, the boy said, "So what happened to the state secrets?"

They were there, sewn, each day's accretion, into the damask shade of a lamp whose base was an ivory Indian elephant. Nor were we ever to know for what powers they were destined. Neither the spade-beard nor the alp knew, merely the minions of her refulgence. So her plunge carried down with her all her history and intent. The uncle sighed, arose, and shut the great secretary, which seemed to the boy at that moment more than ever the one half of a pyramid jammed against the wall. Thud—sound of the last huge stone that immured King Tut against the ravages of time.

The uncle stooped over the heap of cards and touched to them an imaginary fire. Stand back, boy! The uncle himself heaved back into his chair with something like alarm. See the flames rise, boy, like dark tongues, for this was the last telling.

The uncle contracted a brain fever from which he never recovered, but died a disciplined death, lying on his back, never thrashing or muttering. The mother cooled his forehead with ice packs and forced slivers of ice between his lips, but he never smiled nor opened his eyes. When the doctor lifted his lids to look in, there was nothing there, the old orbs glazed over, insensate.

The mother thought she might stir him by bringing his niece and nephew to the bedside. "Here's the baby and the boy, Uncle 'Lando." She said she saw him try to smile, but the boy knew better. The baby gooed and reached for her brother.

"She's like a rattlesnake," the boy said. "It only strikes at something that moves."

"Hush!"

The father came and chafed the uncle's wrist softly. "Don't try to talk, Uncle 'Lando," he said irrelevantly. "We're right here to take care of you."

The uncle died and was buried. The boy said, "Can I have the cards?" The mother and father looked at each other.

"Yes," said the mother.

The boy took the cards and dropped them into his mind. They sank like the papers he sneaked out of the window at school, slipping and sliding across the currents. It was because they lived in a huge ocean of air, the teacher said, miles and miles deep. Slowly, the cards skittered down to the bottom amid all the other rummage. He could not read the uncle's hand script, but some day he would, and in the meanwhile, he knew what they were about: Gunnar, Ned Brinkin, the Morpheus Man, Little Pio Aguello, and Kristeva, the poisonous obelisk. What frightened the boy was the brevity of Uncle 'Lando's encounter with Kristeva. At supper he said, "Uncle 'Lando didn't see Kristeva but once and he never got over it. How come?"

"That's all the time it takes for femme fatale," the father said.

"What's that?"

"Never mind," said the mother. "If your father tells you everything he knows tonight, you won't have anything to talk about when you grow up."

"Goo. Foo!"

Three days after Uncle 'Lando was buried, the boy took the cards to the alley out back and set them on fire, which brought his father and mother running. The mother had the baby in her arms and hollered, "What do you mean, playing with fire?"

"I'm not playing with fire," said the boy stoutly. "This is what he wanted." That brought the mother and the father up short. They stood gazing dolefully down into the flames, which raced up and down the layers of cards, curling and blackening them.

"Hell," said the father, more with resignation than disappointment. "I thought I might read them some day."

"Goo!" The baby hauled out mightily against her mother's arms to reach the fire. The boy smelled oil and powder on her. It mixed with the incense of the fire. Cinnamon and spice. A tiny deer ran through the fire, all red and bloody. It stumbled and was engulfed. "Oh, Kristeva," wailed the boy, "why did you raise your snow-tipped horns against the law!"

LONERS_____

THE HUNTER

From his vantage on the high ridge the hunter followed the progress of the old woman. Through his gun sight he could see her face clearly—pinched by the cold and deeply lined by exhaustion older than this day's journey. The concave mouth worked hungrily for air. Around the face was a dark wreathing of frayed scarf; below, a black shapeless coat. Boots, black too, shuffled stiffly in the fine first snow. Only the arms made a wide motion, oaring, as though the old woman found some brief purchase in the brittle wind.

At first the hunter was angry, because the old woman was walking straight down the middle of the draw where he had expected the deer to come. Then, biding her slow passage, he became curious. She must, he figured, have come from one of the old Sluice's End cabins. She would have walked across the abrupt low hummocks that they used to think were Indian burial grounds. She must have left her cabin at daybreak to reach the head of the draw by noon, at her pace. Already the hunter could feel the afternoon wind racing down from the mountain, bristling the air, arming it with cat's teeth. The second snow was on its way. It would drive the deer down. If the old woman could hold her pace she would clear the draw before dark. He might get a deer yet. In the meantime the hunter watched and wondered. Why would the old woman undertake such a journey when everybody knew winter was howling in the mountains like a cougar? He studied her face. It was drawn, but it was not the face of starvation. The squinting eyes looked determined all right, but they hadn't calculated the distance right and measured it against those old hobbled legs. The hunter shook his head. Something had affected the old woman's judgment.

The hunter was right about the old woman's miscalculation. She began to yaw. Presently she stepped aside and lowered herself down by the trunk of a pine. The hunter took aim. It was a strange sight. The way the snow had lodged in the bark made the tree trunk look like a big snake with sharply etched scales. The old woman's mouth worked like a guppy's. A prickling commenced on the hunter's neck and ears. It came to him, though he knew it was crazy, that he ought to go ahead and flick off the safety and pull the trigger, because the old woman would never get up again anyway. But he was wrong about that. She did rise and struggle on, though the boots moved slower in the snow and the rowing motion of the arms grew weaker.

IIThe hunter followed cautiously along the top of the ridge. And when the old woman had to stop again and lean against a serpent tree, the hunter crouched and drew up a shrewd smile on his face. "You ain't going to get at me like that, old woman." But the gun grew warm in his hands. The black mouth of the old woman seemed to leech to the gun sight just at the cross hairs. It took an effort for the hunter to lower the gun. The third stop was terrible. The old woman found a rare dark patch on the floor of the draw. She leaned against the sheltering stone that had made it. But a fine snow was beginning to fall, charming the ragged collar of the old woman's coat into a silver fox. That's where he ought to fire, the hunter thought, straight into the heart of the old vixen, painlessly. But the black coat obscured the crosshairs. Suddenly the old woman stiffened convulsively. Her neck strained up, her mouth widened. Then she went slack. Her head fell heavily to one side and she tumbled onto the ground.

The hunter had not fired. In fact, there hadn't been a sound other than the rising wind keening in the neck of the draw. But the buck had heard something, or smelled something. The hunter saw him stop on the rise across the draw, test the wind, then turn and gallop away—a fine young beast with four points. At that moment his coat seemed woven of the white snow and the darkening sky.

The hunter knew, before he reached the old woman, that she would be dead. Still, he thrust his hand down between the two dried old dugs. There was not a tremor of heart beat. She was hardly warm. If he were to open her up as though for dressing, the entrails would hardly steam. But he did find something, a small leather pouch on a stout string. He slipped the string over the old woman's head and weighed the pouch in his hand. It was heavy. Now the hunter had missed his buck. The old woman owed him damages. He opened the pouch and emptied the contents onto the ground. There were a few coins, a negligible sum. The main contents of the pouch were a tiny single-shot pistol and a bag of cartridges. There was a round in the chamber of the pistol. Startled, the hunter carefully removed it. He looked at the old woman's face. Her eyes stared out across the snow. He pulled the lids down, but they slid open again. "Who were you going to get, old woman? Who are you?" He searched the pockets of her coat and dress, but there was nothing to tell who she was. Just an old woman from Sluice's End was all he could tell the sheriff.

He stuffed the pouch in his game pocket and picked up his rifle. But something held his attention, an element of urgency in the stiffening body, as though the legs wanted to push up and the hands claw the jagged air. "Old woman," said the hunter, "who was the hated one that made you misjudge this walk so bad?" The sound of his voice pleased him, the way it struck the big stone and plunged bravely into the wind. "Old woman, if you had written down a name and put it in the pouch, I could've taken care of him for you." He shouldered his rifle and scanned the draw. Snow was veiling the trees and obliterating the crest of the ridge. "It must've been a powerful hatred, old woman."

II

The hunter took no notice of the arrangements the sheriff made. Maybe they took out a pony trap and dragged the old woman back to town. Maybe relatives at Sluice's End claimed her or maybe she had to be buried at public expense. The hunter went about his business of getting three good bucks for the winter. In the spring he would pick off grouse. In the summer were the salmon runs. In the fall the uplands were thick with chukar. That was his life. In his wifeless cabin he set the pouch on the mantel. Presently he noticed a frail breath of foul odor. The pistol was greased with animal fat. He smiled. That was just the way an ignorant old woman would do. He had to scrub it with gasoline. He had to saddle soap the pouch inside and out. And since he had spent so much time in restoration, he decided to wear the pouch and pistol around his neck. It might come in handy in case a logger or an Indian went completely wild at the tavern. But the pouch didn't make the hunter feel safe. Instead, it began to act like a witless lodestone. It drew him through the town, heavy on his neck, bending him down like a pointer. One day it took him all the way out to Juke's mill. "What am I supposed to find?" asked the hunter impatiently. "I can give you the rest of the winter, but not more." The pouch tugged at him, but there was nothing to find. The creek was iced over. The mill wheel was covered with leafless vines. The old house was a skeleton drifted with snow. Old Man Jukes was twenty years dead. Well then, thought the hunter, it was only a pouch of muddled memories. The old woman was addled the day she died, if she was coming to town to shoot Jukes.

So the hunter sat before his fire and chewed venison jerky and carved himself a spare rifle stock. Then the pouch took up a nocturnal life. After supper it would catch the hunter with a sudden heat as though someone had placed a fevered hand on his heart. It would lead him down to the tavern and keep him watching there until the beer and the fire made him too sleepy to keep his eyes open. The tavern keeper laughed. "Why don't you get a wife then, Ames, if you can't stand the long evenings alone."

"I'm looking for somebody, but not a wife."

"Who?"

"A connection of that old woman's that died in the snow last month."

"She didn't have no connections. They inquired out to Sluice's End and they put it in the paper, but nobody came. She was buried a pauper because there wasn't nothing in her cabin worth even the price of a pine box, and who would buy a broke down cabin in Sluice's End?"

"Oh she had connections all right," said the hunter knowingly, but the tavern keeper's picture of the old woman's desolation chilled his bones. "Everybody's got connections somewhere."

"Is that right? Who's your connections, Ames? Suppose I was to find you laid out in the snow."

"You wouldn't have to bury me a pauper. My cabin would bring a price."

"Wouldn't, Ames, unless you had connections. See, there would be lawyers and filings and court and clerk charges until the proceeds wouldn't cover a apple crate and a Indian grave-digger."

The hunter thought about that as he trudged home. It put him in such a black mood that he swore at his cabin and kicked his bed as though they had failed him in some solemn duty. In the days that followed, the pouch yawed like the old woman its owner, dragging the hunter all over town. Out by the depot Indians stared at him. Dogs barked at him in the better parts. Boys peppered him with snowballs. Once it seemed the dry goods store had an attraction, but he refused to set foot in there. At night it was always the tavern. He searched the faces, but they were always the same—heavy loggers, dying old phlegm-spitters, clerks at the pool table, a handful of Indians in the corner. The hunter grew morose and tetchy. One night he slugged a logger and was sent home by the tavern keeper. Another night the tavern keeper said, "There's a new woman named Barstow at the dry goods. If I was you I would go court her. Or you can sit around here and go rancid."

The hunter stomped out of the tavern. But the next afternoon he went to the dry goods store and spoke to the Barstow woman. She was under forty, and not too roughed over by the winters. "Miss Barstow," he said.

"Missus." She smiled.

"Widow?"

"Widow."

"Widow Barstow, I want leave to court you in the spring."

She shook her head. "I don't want a man if his sap dries up in the winter."

"It ain't that."

"What is it then?"

"I made a promise for the winter."

"Then go back to her." Her face flamed up.

"I can't. It's a dead woman."

"That's even worse. I can't fight the dead."

"And you won't wait until spring?"

"I might have to, and beyond, but not willingly, not while I have eyes to cast about."

"Then I'll come tonight. Where do you live?"

"Right above your head."

Suddenly the hunter felt a chill breath on his face. The pouch steadied, stone cold. He said, "You don't know who I am."

"You're Ames, the hunter. But you haven't asked me what I want for a present."

"What is it?"

"Sherry wine."

"Sherry wine," he repeated, but his mind was not on the words because the snow forest had entered the room. The light dimmed. The color drained from the Barstow woman's face and she receded greatly in distance. The hunter found himself looking through his gun sight. The cross hairs roamed in the dark shadow the woman made on the snow and then steadied on her throat. "Eight o'clock," she said.

"Eight o'clock."

When the hunter got back to his cabin his eye was clear, but he was in the grip of fear. He paced the room, remembering how in the dry goods store the pouch had gone cold and how the sight had steadied on the Barstow woman's throat. He shook his fist. "You're crazy as hell, old woman. I'm through with you. I bury my oath." He stamped on the floor as though he were tamping a murderer's grave. "It's all off." He seized the pouch string, but he could not pull it from his neck. He wrestled it as though it were a serpent, until he fell to the floor panting. When he dropped his hands, the string grew loose again. He drew his knife from its sheath, but he could not cut the string. A palsy shook the knife from his hand. He lay in his bed and looked up at the dark cage of rafters. "Well then, old woman, you've got me, but I won't take your revenge. Do what you can." He half expected the strings to wind and strangle him or the pouch to freeze his heart, but they did not.

Later, he walked to the liquor store and then to the widow's room. She poured the wine into a crystal decanter. From the decanter she filled two small tulip goblets. She sat across a small table from him and proposed a toast. "To a successful courtship."

"I'm afraid it can't be," he said.

She smiled. "Why?"

They sipped. "Because the old woman has hold of me."

"Tell me about the old woman."

"You won't believe it," he said

"I'll believe it," she said, sitting straight in a dark velvet dress that almost hid the shadow of her full breasts.

So the hunter told her everything, not omitting even the way in which the cross hairs had steadied on her throat three hours ago. He watched her face carefully and when he had finished his story he said, "What was between you and the old woman?"

"You."

"Me? I never knew either of you."

"You knew us." She stepped around the table and unbuttoned the collar of his shirt. She looked at the pouch and touched it and then she returned to her chair. "So I am the one."

The hunter nodded solemnly. "But I won't kill you. I told the old woman so."

The widow, to his surprise, took no interest in his promise. She said, "It took you first to old Juke's mill?" He nodded. "What did you see there?"

"Wreckage and snow and a frozen creek."

"What did you see in the creek?"

"I saw a ripe old dog-salmon laboring under the ice. I saw my face."

She leaned across the table until their faces were very close. "What do you see in my eyes?" Her breath made a warm sweetness in his nostrils. "What do you see?" she said. What he saw was a broad-faced boy, flushed, his eyes narrow with mirth. "A boy," he said. But it was not a boy, it was himself—as he might appear in a silver ball on a fancy stand in a rich man's yard. "You must have been a rich man's wife," said the hunter, looking again at the crystal decanter and the tulip goblets.

"Maybe I was." Then she said, "We can break the old woman's hold."

"I doubt it."

"Yes we can. I want you to come back tomorrow at this time. I want you to do exactly what I say. Do you promise?"

"I promise."

All that night and the following day the hunter suffered greatly. The coldness of the pouch was almost unbearable. He was afraid his heart would freeze. He knew what the old woman was saying—that if only he would fire the pistol into the Barstow woman's throat all would be well. But the Barstow woman had said she could break the old woman's hold. The hunter fervently hoped so, because what would he do if she couldn't?

He went to her room that night. She smiled as she let him in. "Don't look so black." She led him to the same small table. And now he knew she had been a rich man's wife. She wore a long white gown lacey and open above the breast. It was made of many thin layers and was tied at the waist with a silk sash. It was embroidered with shiny white flowers like edelweiss in the snow. When she sat across from him, the gown opened like a morning flower and revealed the knee and calf of one leg. A fierce battle began in the hunter between the heat of his desire and the chill of the old woman's pouch. The Barstow woman poured the tulip goblets full of sherry wine. She held hers out and touched it to his with a tiny ring. When they had sipped, she said, "Is she tormenting you?"

"Yes."

"You remember your promise?"

"Yes. But you better hurry and break her hold."

The Barstow woman nodded. She got up and walked to her bed. The hunter didn't remember having seen the bed the night before, and yet how could he have forgotten it? It had high posts, a white canopy, and curtains. The hunter was muddled. The wine and the Barstow woman's dazzling fineries made him dizzy. Who was she? Where was he? And what was it she was saying?

"Take out the pistol?"

"Yes, take out the pistol and load it." As he opened his collar and loosened the mouth of the pouch, she said, "Can you remember a deer that you killed well, without pain?"

"Yes."

"Can you aim like that again?"

He snapped the cartridge chamber shut and lifted the pistol. She looked upward. Her mouth opened and her throat worked gently. He wondered if she were singing. But all he could hear was the wind stiffening. The scudding snow began to cover her coat and the rock behind. The hunter feared he could not get a clear shot. Melting flakes caused the cross hairs to waver. But at length the sight steadied. He fired. A dark blossom leaped to her throat, probably crimson, but he could not be sure in that driving snow. The hunter removed the pouch and dropped it at his side along with the pistol. Lightness and relief drowsed him so thoroughly that he could not resist sleep, dangerous as he knew it was in the snow. While he slept he heard the old woman. At first he thought it was only her death rattle, but it was more like a crooning, like the last sweet bubbling in the deer's throat under the knife. He expected silence to come, but it did not. Instead, the crooning went on and on.

The hunter awoke. The wind had died. The snow fell so evenly that it was like seeds broadcast by a careful sower. He saw where the love-sick crooning came from—the old woman's bower of snow. It lay before him in the near distance at the end of a short path. It was a deadly beautiful thing with curtains of frost, swags of snow, and pinnacles of ice. But the coldest of all was the love-sick crooning which froze the hunter's groin.

Presently he began to weep, which unmanned him. So he wiped the tears savagely on his sleeve and unsheathed his knife. He knew what the old woman had done—tricked him into killing the Barstow widow, then taken her place. The hunter went forward, knife uplifted. He would plunge it immediately, he would not give her time to freeze him with her eyes. He threw aside the white curtain. But he did not strike. It was not the old woman under his knife but the widow. She was naked except for a green velvet choker that held a rose in the center of her throat, a rose that throbbed ever so slightly as she sang. The hunter's passion blazed—and mounted more and more as he saw in the liquid of her eyes his clothes drop one by one from his body, saw his own face broad and boyish. But even as there stirred in him motions he had not remembered for years, something else awed him more—her body. It was firm and even muscular, just as he had imagined. It was the widow's. The breasts were large and the nipples ruddy, for they had been often kissed and caressed. But something had removed the marks of the cold country. Something had stripped away all the winters, as though a hand had peeled one by one the layers of her white gown. That was the only magic—not the boyish quickening of his blood, not the fatal shot that was only a rose, not even the strange sisterhood of the old woman—but only this, the winterless body and bower of the widow which now he entered.

BEASTS

She sat to her pad by a wall where the wintry afternoon sun slipped the spires of fir and made through the window a golden rectangle. As the day declined, the golden box ascended into the louring dark of the rafters. Then she went down and made supper for Michael.

Michael was not the one she was trying to draw. The one she was trying to draw was utterly different—not just in lineaments, bones, or ligature, but deeper, where tiny firings directed the order and latching of cells. She didn't speak of this to Michael. He would scoff. Michael, his hands slick with salmon milt and eggs, was a realist.

It was not duty that sent her down from pad to kitchen, nor the cold at the margin of the sun, the frigid air marching down from the Arctic as precise in its claims of continent as etcher's acid. What sent her down was each day's exact bight of time. She imagined there turned above her in the sky the wheel of a huge machine that caught in its starbright teeth Time. If the sketching went well, the wheel made a regular ticking. If it went badly it tocked and tightened, a Catherine Wheel stretching and cracking her nerves. Either way, it was good to stand aside and look up into the blue sky where soon her creature would appear on the great pennons of his coming. Especially good after a false start. Once she had sketched something between Fra Angelico and Blake, a cherubic muscleman for a celestial pageant, a sadly comic miscarriage.

In the kitchen Michael said, "How's it going?" crossing his feet on the table, showing the deeply treaded bottoms of his boots, which would've angered her, but she felt an unexpected surge of pity for this earthbound creature stomping about, waffling the fragile snows of December, imagining he had power.

"Coming," she corrected.

"All right. What's coming down, as the hippies say?"

"If I already knew, I wouldn't have to paint it."

He laughed. "If it's coming, it's coming. Not much you can do about it, is it?"

"Well. Listen to the great artificial inseminator. You think the salmon have forgotten how to propagate?"

"That's different, and you know it. Man has decimated the runs. Now he has to build them back up."

Ever so often Michael would come up at the end of the day and look at the pad. "When are you going to stop sketching and start painting?"

"When it's time."

She knew she was a mystery to him. When they made love he probed her cruelly. But he couldn't get to the center of her before he shuddered and spent himself. It made her think of the dying fish whose milt he squeezed out over the troughs of amber eggs. Nevertheless, she loved the love-making of her earthen fishy man, because even as he tried to plumb her, his warmth flowed through her and sent her to the loft again, her body hot and throbbing, signaling with its urgent emanations to the creature out there in the winter night, wherever he was. Come.

"When are we going to have a baby?" Michael asked, hoarse from amorous exertion.

"When it's time."

"If you got pregnant you'd start painting. You'd have a natural deadline. You'd know your subject."

"What? A pink baby leaping up over the falls?"

Laughing, he grabbed her and squeezed her until she cried out.

The Day Star beats its way out of Bristol in a brisk sea. Morning breaks. From a bolted chair in his velvet salon the old gentle spies through the port flying fish sailing off the tips of waves, skimming across troughs, playing hide-and-seek among the breakers. The captain comes, clasps his hands behind his back and surveys the watery world outside the port. The old gentleman smiles. "Would that we could fly to our destination like these fish, but we lumber across the sea like a heavy beast. Is this what you seamen call an easy July passage, captain?"

With thumb and forefinger the captain refines the point of his imperial, a black and bristly trencher. "Nobody but a fool predicts the sea, in any season." He steps closer to the port. "And the lowing and bellowing in the hold is enough to waken a sleeping demon. No proper ballast of cargo, so we bob like a cork in a brook." As though to illustrate the captain's figure, the ship slides into a trough and the sea rears up outside the port like an angry mountain.

"Well, we serve our separate masters, captain."

"I am quite sure of mine, sir. Holweck and Sons of London, but I am told that in this enterprise you are your own master."

"Not at all, captain. My master is even more imperative than yours, a whole continent, terra incognita."

"A dark scrabble of continent, I am told, a wilderness of savages."

The old gentleman strikes the deck with his heel making a goodly thump despite the muffling of the carpet. "What do you suppose we sail over this minute, captain? A pretty Atlantis, home to gentle naiads? Nay, rather drear cliffs and valleys with lantern-eyed creatures crawling in the sediment of eons." The old gentleman smiles sharply. "Never imagine, captain, that our real masters are mere men. They are always vastnesses hungering for our occupancy. God knows why, given our composition."

"Does the new continent hunger for these kine that ramp and gore the hold?"

"Indeed, captain. You cannot define a continent without bulls to measure the land and press against the wilderness so that man can come behind." His eyes glitter. "Have you ever seen such splendid kine?"

"They are fine indeed, sir, but if your man does not keep them tight tethered, they will stave in the side and we shall all be pasturing on the ocean floor."

"The bulls are restless because they want to get to the cows."

"Then perhaps we must let them, to restore peace in the hold."

"No. All the new herd must be conceived on the new continent, or we will arrive with creatures standing athwart two worlds and they will be torn in twain."

The ship slides again, creaks, and resounds with a heavy thumping from below.

Whenever she sketched she tied her hair on top of her head, exposing her neck to the air. When she went down to the kitchen she untied her hair. It released a rich odor, as of wet animal. Michael's nostrils flared. The odor came from the sketching. Something got ratted in her hair, something the creature sent in advance of its coming. It stayed until the fragrance of frying scallions, pork, and fresh baked bread took its place.

One day she discovered small signs of disturbance in her dresser drawers—Michael, of course, looking for her pills. But she kept them in a slot between the bottom drawer and the backboard, knowing that they were something he should never see, little nullified eggs nestled coldly in their mechanical wheel. She said, "You better stay out of my things. Don't you know what happens to men who meddle in women's mysteries?"

Michael shrugged. "I want us to have a baby."

"So do I, but not yet."

"Not until the great canvas is painted, right? But God knows when that will be."

"Well, you can stretch the canvas now. I'm nearly through sketching." Actually that was not true, or she hadn't known it was true. But his vehement yearning had wrenched it from her.

"How big do you want it?"

"Big enough so that seven sleepers could float one above the other in tiers."

"Tomorrow I'll drive to Skagmer to get the canvas and some two-by-sixes for the frame and struts."

She imagined herself mixing paint on a big palette. She would have to stand on the kitchen stool to reach the top of the canvas. But she couldn't see yet the creature she would be painting. And this absence went to the pit of her stomach, a nauseous balloon of effete gas.

"What's the matter?"

"Black," she said. "The first thing I'll mix is black and lay on a layer at the top."

"Sure, paint the whole canvas black if you want to and the other stuff on top."

"The paints are going to cost a lot. I'll have to order them from Seattle."

He shrugged. "We don't spend much out here."

That caused her to look down at herself—at the heavy calf-high boots, the long black dress with high neck and full sleeves, the dirty white apron, and the only visible parts of her body, hands and wrists, more bone than flesh. If she were in front of a mirror, she would see a face also long and prominent of bone—sharp chin, high cheeks, and a forehead as broad as a griddle. She laughed sharply.

"You certainly are acting queer."

"I am queer. Did you expect some ordinary woman to come up here and live with you at a salmon hatchery a hundred miles from nowhere? Draw all day in a cold attic, cook supper and ball every night?" She paused and smiled inwardly. "It probably has to do with the birches and alders and river rocks."

"What's that supposed to mean?"

"It means I'm big-boned and pale white. I probably mistook them for my kin."

"You don't smell like a rock or a tree."

"What do I smell like?"

"You smell like a woman."

After supper Michael said, "Make a list of the art supplies you need. We can drive down to Seattle and pick them up if you want to."

"No. I'll order by mail. If I went down to Seattle and saw the space needle and all the pretty people, I might never come back."

The sea outside the port of the velvet salon no longer breaks. Instead, mountainous ground swells loom over the ship as though they would whelm her, only to disappear with a precipitous drop that causes the old gentleman's stomach to churn up an unpleasant gas. "So," he says, "we are seeing the tail end of the storm."

"Aye, of this storm," says the captain, his eye fixed on the louring sky outside the port. "But two days hence, I warrant, we'll be reefing sails, throwing out a sea anchor, and wishing we had a cargo of iron instead of kine." He looks now not at the old gentleman but at a figure standing beside him, the pastor of the herd, dressed all in leather—jerkin, britches, greaves and buskins. "How taut, herdsman, can you tether those beasts? If I told you that in the coming storm the shifting of the herd as much as two feet would topple us, could you save us?"

The pastor has a keen monkeyish face with sharp eyes.

"Nay not a yard, herdsman, but two little feet and down we go, hull over mast, to the bottom of the sea. What can you do, herdsman?"

"We ne'er tether 'em so close at home, sir, but I warrant it can be done."

"Must be done. Trice them up and batten them as tight as prisoners in the stocks."

"They'll not stand easy for it."

"Damn their ease, herdsman. See that it's done, for if I know the storm that lurks beyond the horizon, we will hang on inches. Go below. I will send the carpenter. What more you need of stanchions he will furnish. If he can shore up a battered bulkhead, he can shore up a bull, by God. And I will send you the bosun with a quantity of good hemp."

The old gentleman says, "What of Curran, pastor?" He turns to the captain. "Curran is the master bull of the herd. I fear such restraint will madden him and that his bellowing will madden the others."

"Very likely, sir," says the pastor.

The captain grimaces. "Then we shall sling him with a double sheet of sail and hoist him up with a cargo block. The carpenter will rig it for you. I have it on good authority that a slung beast with no purchase on the earth will settle quite nicely. The airy suspension and the swaying return him to his mother's womb. But if he like it not, he will nevertheless be up out of the way and his weight will not shift."

"Very well then, sir." The pastor, excuses himself and goes to his charges in the hold below. Here are seven bulls and forty cows, stalled as if in a barn, each bull separately, the cows in pairs. Straw lies thick on the deck. Bails of hay are lashed to the outboard bulkheads. The odors of timothy and dung thicken the air. The pastor breathes deeply, then assumes an antic posture of intense vigilance, holding his cupped hands to his eye like a long glass and sweeping the offing. "Ho now, lads and lassies, what do I spy? Sleek herds of whales and manatees pasturing, bull and cow, in the great Sargasso Sea." He lowers his imaginary glass and knits his brows like a child aping a deep thinker. "Why then, it matters not, lads and lassies, whether we swim in air or water, for both are rich in fodder." He threads his way among the stalls like a clever fish through a treacherous weir until he comes to the great bull Curran and whispers in his ear. "We must swing you up, lad, like a flying fish." The bull grows restive and tosses his horns at the pastor, who laughs. "But you would rather be mounted up on one of these fine cows, eh lad." The pastor dashes away among the cows, leaps onto the back of one and shouts, "How about this comely lass, my man," and bounces until the patient beast lows its displeasure.

At the loft window she performed an old trick of eye and imagination, putting together things inside her head with things outside the window. The firs brushed an electric cobalt cloud never before seen from this planet. The hatchery creek ran over a blanched bed more like weathered bone than basalt, never before seen in any sublunary landscape. Next, under the rippling refractions of a sky-blue wash, she ran Michael through the montage of his duties—feeding azure fingerlings in the troughs, counting cerulean returns by the trap pond, squeezing out eggs and milt in the plumy mist of the incubation house, taking the lunch she'd packed him downstream below the fish ladder, where bears contended with the eagles that dropped from the sapphire sky to feast on ripe salmon in the shallows.

Tomorrow Michael was going into Skagmer to get canvas and lumber and check at the post office to see if the paints and brushes had come up from Seattle. She should be making final sketches, but she put on her coat and left the house. She wandered out to the fingerling troughs. At her approach the fish whirled in a single body and swam away to the far end. That was the trouble with fish. They had no sense of individuality, schooling as if they were one eternal body only temporarily broken up by earthly life. She went to the incubation house, warm and moist under its membrane of clear plastic. How plangent in this enclosed place the trickle of water over the tiny alevins nested in their gravel beds. She looked down into the long pan. The bright little amber bodies were just beginning to elongate, each with its vivid though still undifferentiated black eye. She felt the urge to take a stick and scramble these embryonic creatures, produce some radical mutation, let it be monstrous even, anything but this endless uniformity. What was the sense of life reproducing itself over and over in the same shapes? Still, the little black eyes riveted her, tightly clustered there in the gravel, already forming the enchainment of interlocking lives that guaranteed their common destiny.

Back in the house she went to her dresser and took out the pills from their secret cache—three wheels of them, two full, one almost empty. How lifeless and mechanical they looked, each little beige round in its place. She took them to the kitchen and dropped them into the trash.

She went to the loft and took up her pad. Was there any meaningful image there amid the dozens of unfinished sketches? Some elemental shape struggling up out of the scrabble of pencil scratch? She thought there might be—a big indeterminate black thing suspended in an erratic scrabble of ground strokes, a strenuous thrusting up of something not naturally airborne. But, my God, what a clumsy black mass it was. If the firs themselves had tried to fly, dragging roots and clots of soil, they couldn't have looked more inept. And yet there was some fiercely yearning power driving the thing toward the shores of light. Her mind skittered off crazily to Michael, the dark incontinent beast that descended on her almost nightly.

She closed the pad and mused. Outside the window the light diminished in the garden of fish and the clouds loured gray over Mt. Kilshin. A motion caught her eye—Michael coming up from the river, a deep shadow on his face. No, it wasn't a shadow. It was hair, a beard. My God, he'd gone down river among the bears and grown a beard in a single afternoon. She shook her head, blinked her eyes, and fixed her gaze on him as he approached. It was there all right, the beard. She hurried down to the kitchen.

The carpenter and the bosun have come and gone, and now the hold is a congeries of ropes, stanchions, and crossbars as intricately woven as a weir, stay and stall, a primordial maze into which the beasts have wandered and lost themselves. Even the block and sling hanging over the great bull Curran with its thick hemp falls seems a pendent of old Nature, vinous and serpentine, from that time when vegetative and animal were undifferentiated.

The herd is relatively quiet now, subdued by the bewildering increase of objects that separate them, ropes that fetter them. The pastor perches on a high crosspiece. "Well, how like you, lads and lassies, to be trussed up like dangerous outlaws? Methinks you would not bear it so peaceable if I had not mixed a little drowsy-weed with your timothy. 'If a cow go foraging in the sea, how very cautious she must be, lest the fishes lure her to the pit.' Eh?"

The ship rolls steeply. The pastor hunkers down. "But are we already in the pit, lads and lassies? The sky is dark at noon. The captain, the carpenter says, does not like the ship's moment. The cargo disturbs it. That's us. But I never meant to meddle with the ship's moment. Did you? Let her have whatever moment she pleases, I say." He rubs his face vigorously as if to remove a tacky web of confusion. "Still, methinks we will come out of this pit of night, lads and lassies, for we have a destiny in a new continent and the old master has a compact with the Powers."

Up in the velvet salon, shuddering now in the onset of the tempest, the captain has made his report to the old gentleman. The storm may be worse even than he feared.

"I am not afraid, captain. I trust you. And I think a storm is not a very high thing." He receives a curious look from the captain. "I mean that a storm reaches not to the heavens. Some day we will teach ourselves to go up high and then we will see that a storm is only a little eddy in the great airy river of our sky."

"That may be, sir, but today we are down here on the sea's surface, God help us." He hastens up the ladder to the bridge.

"Godspeed, captain." The old gentleman rolls and pitches in his bolted chair. Violent water claws at the port. Still, the old gentleman's face is mildly bemused. "Well, Curran, I believe the continent wants us more than the sea, though I grant you it's a devil of a sea. You in your airy sling will fly us to land and there we will find green and gold as far as the eye can see." A towering wave crashes over the ship, rattling the old gentleman's teeth. For once he looks displeased. "Oh thunder on, vain tempest! My herd and I have a destiny beyond your greedy maw."

In the kitchen she said, "OK, where'd you get the beard?"

Michael looked at her in angry amazement. "By God, you really haven't noticed, have you? I thought you were just stonewalling me."

"Why didn't you say something instead of sneaking off and getting it on the sly?"

"It grew out of my face, goddamit, while you were up in the attic dreaming." He pulled on some of the longer hairs, raising the flesh of his face into little peaks. "See?"

"That doesn't prove a thing. A magic beard would obviously go to great lengths to look natural."

He eased himself slowly into his chair, never taking his eyes off her, like a gunfighter.

"It would also create a false memory of growing. But I can tell you that today, like every other day, I washed your little black hairs out of the bathroom sink." She smiled. "Well I shouldn't be mad. Hair is a universal curse. I was supposed to be your pure birch-bark river-rock woman, but this stinking hair came on my head and elsewhere, and I couldn't do a thing about it." She sighed. "I'll start supper. We hairy beasts have to eat."

Michael hoisted his feet up on the table and looked across the room. Sleet lashed the window and battened itself on the panes.

Three days later, after much sawing and hammering, there stood— stretched, framed, and braced—a canvas seven feet high and half again that long. Also provided by Michael were an easel and a spring-loaded stool on casters that rolled into place and then locked when you stood on it. On a table, come from Seattle, was a great jumble of palettes, brushes, paints, and solvents.

"Thank you," she said. But when he'd gone away, she could hardly move. It wasn't just the daunting task. The room had changed—the light muted, the ticking of the sky wheel muffled. Was it because she'd thrown away the wheels that governed her fertility? No. Something had come into the room, and not just the canvas. She looked around. But she didn't need to see it. She knew it was the clumsy urgent thing struggling up from the scrabble of strokes in her pad. She squeezed some black paint on a palette, but she couldn't begin. Standing in front of the canvas, she grew dizzy. The room yawed. The sun outside the window got tangled in the firs and threw on the wall a wild thicket of crazed light. The floor shifted under her feet. She had to drop down on her haunches to keep from falling.

"Well, did you lay on some black?"

"No. I squatted down with my butt touching the floor."

"Why? Is it going to be one of those Dali pictures where you're looking up at everything?"

"No. I squatted because I was dizzy. I think maybe I'm pregnant. I got off the pill a few days ago."

Michael's eyes brightened and he came toward her.

"Don't, for God's sake, hug me or something stupid like that. It wasn't you that got me pregnant."

"Who was it?"

"The one up in the attic, your leader—Shadow Man, Smoke Man, Cloud Man—whatever you warlocks call him. He's still cruising around up there. I had to get down on my haunches to keep from getting knocked flat. Who can paint?"

Michael said nothing.

"You're not even listening, you hairy oaf. All you're thinking about is the baby, isn't it? A big pink baby jumping over the falls."

Sea and sky have converged on the ship, the twin furies of air and water now one indistinguishable black howling. In the hold hangs the great bull Curran under a creaking block. Suspended in canvas sheets, he has at last stopped bellowing and is reduced to a slaverous moaning. The other kine are conquered by fear, the wide-eyed cows lowing piteously, the frothy bulls tossing their horns in aimless frenzy. The deck is awash with sea water that sluices in contrary currents through the legs of the beasts like a mountain stream gone crazy.

The pastor scuttles with monkey-like agility here and there among stanchions and bars, checking knots and fittings, stopping to soothe with words and hands a particularly distraught beast. Through several long hours now of cruel buffeting the herd has held fast. But suddenly the girth line on one of the bulls parts. He shifts clumsily with the roll of the ship. The strain on the other ropes is too great. Leg lines and halter snap. The beast careens across the deck, braces himself, survives one roll but stumbles wildly down the next, crashes into the bulkhead, and brains himself. Down he goes, blood gushing from his mouth and darkening the swirling sea water.

In the blink of an eye the pastor snatches a coil of line from a cleat on the bulkhead. A loose beast could stave a hole in the side of the ship. So, when the bull slides through the wash and thumps to a stop against a stanchion, the pastor begins an astonishingly rapid and skillful lacing, like a spider trussing a fly up in its web. Thus, before the ship shifts again, the dead beast is immobile, lashed to the post. The pastor cinches the rope, cuts loose the remainder of the coil, and moves rapidly among the herd looking for other weakened lines.

Up in the salon the old gentleman has triced himself in his chair. The port has been shaken loose by the storm. Sea and rain stain the carpet. Nevertheless, the old gentleman wears a look of furious determination, seems ready to fling defiance at the gale, when suddenly there comes such a horrible cracking and crashing that even he loses color. A shout from above, though broken by the wind, informs him that the mizzenmast is down. He imagines the catastrophe. For long hours the great timber has bent patiently under the cruel blasts of the storm, its reefed sail faithfully keeping the ship pointed upwind. Through shuddering plunges and huge sweeps of gale that have heaved the stern and rudder entirely out of the water it has stood fast. But then comes a contrary swirl of air, the absence of all pressure, followed instantly by the next heavy gust.

Out billows the sail and down comes the timber. It was the absence, not the blast, that ferreted out the one weak grain in that noble heartwood. The rigging parts as though it were gossamer. The sail drops. The deck hands leap to the life lines, but one luckless seaman slips, tangled in the rigging, and dies under the crashing timber.

The old gentleman does not allow the vision to occupy his mind. The hullabaloo out on deck fades from his ear, the drear cliffs and gorges of ocean from his eye. In their place he envisions the great bull Curran sailing high above the storm. Below, the green-gold globe turns in slow rotation, the storm only a tiny gray wheel on the blue ocean, a dog chasing its tail. "Oh, incontinent storm, give up your bluster. I and my herd are destined for a wide green land. Give it up!"

In the cold clean air of the loft she smelled her own must. These last days she had not bathed. Michael didn't care. Whether you were fragrant or high, Michael was your man.

The black thing was there somewhere, though she couldn't see it. She looked out the window. Was it hanging under the eaves like a huge sloth slewing its dark eyes toward her? No. That was only a subterfuge she made up. The only way to get hold of it was to paint it. She squeezed a big glob of black onto a palette and rolled a long-handled brush in the pigment until it was a stake with a glistening knob, a pitchpole. But the moment she touched brush to canvas, the fabric began to quiver and whine, the very opposite of the ticking of the great wheel that had once regulated her days. What caused the quivering? Maybe Michael in screwing together the timbers had inadvertently created a torque sensitive to touch. No. It was impossible that Michael could make anything misshapen—crude, yes, but not misshapen.

She gathered her will and stabbed an inky smudge onto the canvas. The trembling fabric, quickening to her brush, caused the edge of black paint to frizzle electrically. And there in her mind's eye was Michael looking over her shoulder. "You crazy bitch, you made me put all this stuff together so you could paint a cunt!" And then his coarse braying laugh. She was glad when he was gone. But in some odd way the gust of laughter helped. A figure began to take shape in the smoky recesses of her imagination.

The figure sat cross-legged, stupefied by the smoke rising up under the tripod from the cleft in the rocks. Grossly painted she was—a greenish bar for a hair line, eyes blue welts, nose and mouth black holes, neck beaten bronze, nipples and aureoles the twin heads of a coiled serpent, the omphalos an umber vortex. In her mouth she mumbled laurel, gums cold and numb. So where was the oracle to come from, the vivid politic metaphor the priests needed to report to their masters? The painter laughed. From the nether lips of course, whose whisperings could be glossed according to the hermeneutical necessities of the state. And then she stopped laughing. Because she saw that the sibyl with her skeletal protuberances was herself. And she thought: all these weeks to paint a self-portrait of the woman of the rocks? Not on your life! She smutched the canvas with black crisscrosses.

She walked over to the window and looked down into the winter fish garden. All was quiet by the troughs and the green shed. But a tear must've risen in her eye, because there against her lower lid belled an image of Michael. He was dressed in a bear skin, very realistic except that the headpiece was awry and she could see his bearded face within. Also the fur swagged heavily on his legs. Had he killed the animal and skinned it out, or had he borrowed it from a medicine man? But what silly game was he playing, first a beard, now a bear? He went to the trough of larger fingerlings, cocked his head warily—very realistic she conceded—and then scooped out a little wriggler with his paw and dropped it down his gullet. She smiled to think of the fish wiggling inside the bearskin. This was repeated several times. Then, pretending animal cunning, he ran on all fours toward the creek—to throw the fish in the holding pond no doubt.

Later, in the kitchen, she complimented him. "Very convincing. I almost thought it was actually a bear."

"Thought what was actually a bear?"

"You at the trough in your suit, eating fish. How'd you know I'd be looking?"

Michael smiled. "You're pregnant. You couldn't be acting so crazy unless you were pregnant."

"All right then, if it was a real bear, why didn't the skin fit?"

Michael was grinning now. "Maybe it was that big black guy that's been cruising the attic. Pretty soon you'll be eating grubs and clay, you know."

"All right, if it was a real bear, why don't you get your gun and shoot it. Ha!"

"If it was a real bear I'll have to, or she'll rob us blind."

"She!"

In the salon the old gentleman is asleep in his chair. The ropes he bound himself with still circle his chest, but loosely. The captain comes and wakes him. There is a sharp smile above his imperial. The old gentleman returns the smile, but stiffly, still weary from the rigors of the storm. "It sounds to me, captain, as though the storm is dying."

"The storm has gone one way and we another." Outside the port the light brightens and the waves roll almost gently. "By noon we shall see an azure welkin, as the poets have it."

"All thanks to you, captain. No other master could have guided us through that wretched pudder, which is why I contracted with Holweck for you and no other."

"It was mostly good fortune, sir. When the mizzenmast went down and we had little hope of keeping upwind, why then suddenly the storm abated and we came out by our skins."

"No. It was you, captain. A sibyl came to my dream and showed me how when the mizzen fell and our fortune went all aflutter, then down came the blade of your beard, spiked itself into the deck, and held us upright in the raging sea. Dreams, however strange, never lie, captain, if you know how to read them, as the ancients knew." The old gentleman pauses. "The only misfortune, it seems, was a little blood."

"One of the bosun's men and one bull, not Curran."

The old gentleman sighs. "You could not expect to get through that tempest wholly unscathed. God rest them, man and beast. Soon we shall smell earth and be free of these toppling mountains of water."

"Aye, sir. We should see landfall in a week if the wind holds and we raise the mizzen again."

The old gentleman is pensive. "I know, captain, you must have thought that our irregular cargo and barbarous destination doomed the ship."

"I will not lie to you, sir. I did think something like that and in the wildest hour of the tempest cursed you and your kine, God forgive me."

"Quite understandable, captain, but all the while the opposite was true. My herd is destined for the continent by a power higher than the sea's anger."

Both men are silent. The bellow of a bull sounds distantly.

Could the old gentleman witness the scene in the hold at that moment, he perhaps might modify his pensive smile. The pastor is slowly lowering Curran with the windlass the carpenter has mounted on the bulkhead. Tock! Tock! Tock! The teeth of the windlass measure line to the descending beast. Below, the stall is not empty. A cow stands there, wild-eyed, looking up at Curran. Moments later the bull's hooves touch the deck and he surges up on the cow with a triumphant bellow. It requires all the pastor's agility to snatch away lines and girdle of sail before they become entangled between the two beasts.

Through the herd runs a restive lowing. Quickly, the pastor leaps up on a crossbar. "Hst! Hst!" He coils like a serpent, ready to spring. The kine grow quieter and quieter until finally there is only the slaverous noise of the rutting beasts, the moan of the cow, the stertorous huffing of the bull. The pastor smiles. "Fear not, lassie. When you calve on the new continent, old master will ne'er be the wiser."

After supper Michael got out his rifle. She hated the sight of it—blued barrel, black hole. "Well, if you'd frightened her away before she got a taste of fish you would've saved her."

She said nothing to that but went on washing her plates. They were bone-white stoneware, thick, with good heft. She imagined the suave feel of the white clay. She hummed loudly. The humming contained many things—the kiln that fired the plates, the wheel that ticked in the loft, the sibyl that mumbled laurel, the canvas that quivered on its tripods under the weight of the coming beast.

In the morning, as she cleared the breakfast things, Michael the hunter appeared smiling outside the kitchen window, mouthed a kiss, and said, "Goodbye, little mama. See you at supper." His words, warbled by the window glass, sounded intolerably silly. She couldn't force herself to give him back a smile.

She went to the loft and confronted the quivering canvas with its slashes of black. OK, the sibyl was a mistake. The sibyl was only the keeper of the entrance. The thing to be painted was below the cleft, where the gods had carved a vast hold, an inverted sky, black instead of blue, but fecund, humming with life. That's where the black beast was. But how could you paint what you couldn't see? How paint an inversion? The hue on the opposite side of color?

She stepped back, and there in the window was the bear shambling amiably up the path to the fish garden. She could've opened the window and scared it off, but she didn't. So the beast came to the trough and dipped, almost daintily, among the fish and brought up a slice of wriggling silver and slipped it between bright teeth. And then it came, the brutal report. And down went the bear. But it was far more than the bear that fell. The whole tapestry of mountain fell. Down went alderwood, creek, white rock, fish garden, everything. In its place rose a bleared grayness swimming with hot tears, and after that blackness. So Michael had shot down the world as only a brash fool could. And all the more damnable because he was still there, triumphant in the destruction he visited on them, rolling the dead beast up onto a skid, dragging it off to the edge of the woods, skinning it, dressing it, finding under his knife the embryonic shapes of cubs.

She fell to the loft floor and began to contract. Her fingers folded into her palms. Her knees pulled up under her chin. Her head bent down. Her toes curled. And all her organs knotted together. A stinking compact of dead animal matter. Let the mighty hunter dress that.

But after a while life had its way. A potent heat spread through her. She began to pant and sweat. She rolled up onto her haunches, stood. Her breath came in hot gusts. She couldn't stand her clothes. She pulled off sweater and dress and threw them swirling across the room. She unlaced her boots, pulled them off, threw them against the wall, pulled off her socks. Now all that encumbered her was the winter underwear, neck to thigh. She unbuttoned it, fingers working nimbly, and moments later she peeled it off. Free. No, not quite. Her hair. She pulled out the combs and flung them aside. From the floor she heard clothes and combs make the plaintive chittering of abandonment.

She found brush and palette, tube of black, took them up and advanced toward the canvas. Scraps of the light that Michael had shot out of the sky returned to glisten in the paint. She descended into the mouth below the crone, painting her black way along the slick membrane of the gullet, inch by inch, minute by minute. Tick. . . tick . . . tick.

Michael came up and found her, white, translucent in moonshine. He watched her plunge forward toward the canvas, lay on a few strokes and then leap away as though driven back by the claws of some ferocious animal.

"Jesus Christ! You going to bay at the moon?"

She said nothing to that.

He touched her. "You're freezing."

She shook him off. Her hair fluttered tensely over her shoulders, something black flown in out of night.

The Day Star keeps her westerly course, the wind light but steady on the starboard quarter. The crushed sailor has been committed to the sea. The galley cooks have butchered the bull and made of it fine roasts and pasties to fete the crew, heroes of the storm. The splintered stump of the mizzenmast has been uprooted and a second base newly cut and collared. The pole is raised to a great cheering. There is an almost inebriate joy, a mid-ocean May Day. The shouts of the seamen are full of high joviality. Up in the rigging they fairly dance in place.

The old gentleman stands by the captain on the poop deck not far from the wheel. His eyes brighten mischievously. "Too bad we don't have some maids for this ceremony, captain."

The helmsman smiles guardedly, but his caution is insufficient. "Mind your helm!" barks the captain. Then turning to the old gentleman: "I'm afraid there would be the devil to pay, sir."

"Perhaps not, if they were naiads, mermaids, untouchables of the deep. Can you command the attendance of such?"

"No, nor would I if I could, sir. These ruffians are better fit for a storm than a lady's bower."

Presently a concerted hollering goes up, increasing in volume. "What do they want, captain?"

"A bull." The captain picks up his speaking-trumpet and shouts, "No, men, we may not slaughter another bull. They are our cargo, not our provision."

"Not slaughter, sir," booms back a huge seaman, "but decorate as at country feasts. The pastor says it's the custom."

The pastor is there amid the seamen, an odd figure in his tunic, leather britches, greaves, and buskins, smiling impishly.

"Well, what say you, sir? Shall we have a bull to the fest?"

"It meets my approval if the pastor has given his."

The captain tips trumpet to mouth. "You shall have your bull, men, but not until the mizzen is rigged. Why stand ye idle?"

This brings a joyous shout and a great flurry of activity. Stays and rigging are quickly secured. Out of the sail locker comes the mended canvas. Up the mast a seaman nimble as a monkey shimmies with the bitter end of the main-haul, which he runs through the top block and carries back down to the deck. In minutes the sail runs up and bellies with wind. There is a quiet moment while all listen to the mast creak and watch it take the strain. When it is clear that it will hold fast, huzzahs circle the deck.

"May I borrow your trumpet, captain?"

"Certainly, sir."

The old gentleman lifts the trumpet to his mouth. "What are you waiting for, pastor?"

The pastor drops down into the hold. Some moments later he reappears, leading Curran slowly up a ribbed skid. The animal is reluctant and must be urged by halter and horns, whispered to, patted, and cajoled. At last the noble beast steps out onto the deck to the approving shouts of the crew. And here is a minor miracle of provenience, a sudden supply of many-colored rags, which are quickly tied to the bull's horns and swaged over his flanks. The pastor leads Curran about amidst cheers. Some of the younger seamen somersault over the bull's back, but he pays them little mind, suddenly remarkably serene.

"Perhaps," says the captain, stroking his imperial thoughtfully, "he noses the green land."

"Perhaps," says the old gentleman. He looks up into the belly of the sail newly hoisted against the blue sky. In the bosun's stitching of the storm's rents he reads an annunciation, and in the humming of the wind hears a providential song.

She was confidently at work now, mistress of the world of paint. The fir-frayed sun hummed at the window sill on the cusp of March. The sky ticked. Sibyl and hole, beast and hold lay on the same plane. The vanishing point was beyond the sky, or nowhere. Every day she stripped and became a creature of bleached bone, eyes and hair eruptions of shadowless ebony. She crouched before the quivering canvas or leaped up on the stool, laying on black in bold unfeathered strokes. This was the world of inversion. This was the world of the beast.

And she was not just mistress of the loft, but also of the world outside the window, where with her eye she fixed the fish garden, pinioned the scarf of mist against the mountain's throat, froze the firs, locked the schooling of fry in the troughs, prevented all bears. This was her world.

And the thing on the canvas grew in its utter blackness. Oh later there would be margins. There would be blue. Bone white would also be present. There would be red to signify the flush of blood. No beast without blood. In this world black had dominion but not utterly.

One evening she came down from the loft naked, having forgotten to gather up her clothes from the floor. Michael looked up from his chair astonished. Astonishment turned into a rapt gaze.

"Oh." She turned to go back for her clothes.

"Don't." His tone was almost reverent. "Do you paint naked all the time now?"

"Yes."

"You're pregnant."

She looked down to see what signs he had read. Swollen belly? No. Pendant breasts? No. They were as modestly cupped as before. "How do you know?"

"Because your veins are all blue and the light is shining through you."

No. That couldn't be. She needed to be as blanched and planar as a slab of alabaster, flesh and bone fused into one impenetrable white. She was the mistress of the world of paint.

Michael was standing now, aroused, his face flushed, the blood running down under his beard and giving it a ruddy glister. "Would it be dangerous?" His voice was husky with desire.

"Dangerous?" No, it would not be dangerous. But would it be possible? She was bone white and solid with only shadowless strokes of black here and there. All portals inverted, stoppered. She was the mistress of the world of paint.

"To you or the child."

"No."

Michael kissed her gently. "You're cold." He took her by the hand, led her into the bedroom, and tucked her under the covers. He sat on the edge of the bed and undressed, slowly, patiently. But when he stood to turn back the covers he was fully erect. More than erect, she thought—painfully distended. How terrible to be the victim of such desire, the blood beating mercilessly. He took her in his arms and kissed her passionately. He nuzzled her breasts with his beard. He took her nipples in his lips and ran his hand along her inner thigh. Did she warm to him? She thought maybe she did after all. She knew that this wouldn't be like their other love-making. He would not try to prick her and probe her, yearning for a center he could never know. This would be utterly different.

Michael's entry into her was very distant. Michael, poor bear, was there in the bedroom making love to her, loving her with all his heart. But she was in the loft. A fine March wind flew in through the open window. The canvas rippled. The beast of annunciation swept through the room. Still, if she'd had time and voice she would've called down to Michael that she loved, him, loved his fish, that she would come back. But the urgency of the beast was irresistible. Away she went on its back—out over the fish garden with its neat rows of fingerlings, up the ragged flank of Mt. Kilshin, above the misted tree line, up finally above the blanched purity of the mountain's crest. She herself was pure white bone of will. No, not quite—tainted by swatches of black hair and blood-flushed portals. Well, that was inevitable, because when she came back to Michael and the baby she couldn't be closed up like a statue of alabaster.

Now the brightening spring light splayed over her flesh an odd cerise glow that made her want to laugh, the color garish, unpaintable. Away she flew, beyond the mountain, out over a vast continent of green.

THE BIRD WATCHERS

They lived in a small house just back from the road on the west shore of the island. When I first ferried down from town, it was as though they had erected a great canopy of repose or carved it from some secret bay of silence and set it invisibly over their house. On the day of that first visit I discovered its exact dimensions. In the back and along the sides of the lot it pushed boldly against the edge of the dark wood. In the front it sloped down gently just beyond the road, converging at the base of a huge dying fir that clung on the talus of the steep declivity that fronted the tidal flats. It was therefore roughly the shape of an egg, and more than house high, for the wind curled above the chimney without chilling us.

We made daring excursions—down a set of rickety old steps to the flats to contest gulls for clams, out into the forest to a damp hollow where elephant cabbage waved its rank fronds and tiny seedlings sprouted on the mossy carcasses of feeder timber. They watched me enter and exit and enter again the protected zone. They saw that I discovered it but we did not speak of it. We shared my discovery of the transparent grot silently.

And so, before dinner, though we had martinis and I wore a glistening eye and though the old cat sat in my lap like a warm messenger from their hearts, the ovum was not to be spoken of directly. We must skirt. What were their plans, I asked. They wanted to share, with the right kind, of course. They were constructing a bird-feeder. She shooed the cat and he took me to see a table in progress—a roof, a water basin, some troughs—I made out the general outlines.

Later, over brandy, hot and bursting with incipient love, I made a silly speech. I would be their bird man, flying from the frozen North, from my broken marriage and childless house to their hospitable feeder, if they would let me. "Icarian, but inaspirant of the sun," I said pedantically, "low-flying, safely arriving." Of course they wanted me, she said, showing beautiful teeth, slightly gapped, emblem of the erotic carnivore. But I did not covet her. I swear it. I thought fondly of her delicious teeth in his soft flesh, for he was the soft one, wide-bosomed, downy, with gray eyes that tempered the most tumultuous sky. "I will fly down," I said. "Bell the cat."

And then I practiced a delicious abstinence, an aroused and tantric celibacy, coitus semper incipiens, the source, the mad Frenchman says, from Persia through the eastern sea to the Albigensians, of all courtly loves and cults of the rose. It made me gay, passing the phone, touching it, not dialing, for a week and a second week. Then finally, lying in bed in a long concessive passion,

I rang the number and watched the signal run under the sea along the deep cable woven with the images of fishes and the shadows of diving birds. Her voice came back lilting, close, as though it had been waiting just outside my window, hovering on the wind.

On the way down, the ferry was beaten brutally by the sea. Gulls screamed and wheeled brokenly. Islands heaved in the wake like animations of geologic evolutions, mountains aborning. My eyes swam and my stomach rolled. And so I arrived that Sunday in a dark mood. That, I assumed, accounted for my imagining a difference in the ambiance of the zone. It seemed slightly disturbed, from within. And indeed there was a great flutter around the feeder in the back—robins, sparrows, ravens, grossbeaks, and others I cannot name.

The main exhibit of that evening was their collection of bird skulls, which had not yet been unpacked on my first visit. They are yellow, you know, like old ivory, and delicately seamed, as though some fine craftsman had assembled them from carven parts. The nostrils are astonishingly wide, as though they drank great quantities of the wind. And there are deep sockets, too, for big bright eyes. My hostess might herself have been the master craftsman, so knowingly she handled each skull, cradling the fine jaw gently in her palm, avoiding the brittle slope of the skull at the base, a thinness among the small ones even to translucency. She had them displayed on a long shelf covered with linen as blanched and beautifully embroidered as a Christmas altar cloth. The sheen of the raised thread lured the eye into a vinous and flowered labyrinth and then lost it. She had made the cloth to set off and deepen the burnished ebur of the skulls.

Those bones affected me adversely. A joy to my ornithological friends, they were in my eyes more necrotic than beautiful, their fleshless pallor too distinct from the quick dart and eyebright of their recent lives. I turned away. The cat by the fire made a cavernous yawn with bright teeth and presently jumped up into my lap. My hostess told the memorable story of the owl skull, one of the largest and most interestingly configured of the collection.

Her husband was walking in a snowy wood at midnight under a gibbous moon. It was misty, she said, and warm, late in a long winter. The bare branches of the alders made a complex calligraphy against the sky, but the man was not inclined to read its mysteries. He walked slowly, in peace. And then suddenly he was aware of something descending on him. There was scarcely a sharp enough light for a penumbra of wings. But there must have been some mild shadowing of the moon, for he was certain that his first awareness was not of the noise. That came later—the deep flummeting of the great body, pierced by the mounting reedy scream of claws rending the air. The owl was stooping on him as though he were a small creature darting in the snow. The man crouched and dodged instinctively, but the owl struck his shoulder, and they tumbled together into the snow. The man lay senseless for some moments. When he came to he was frightened for his life because it seemed to him that the woods and the sky had set upon him some dark avenger. For what crime? That he disturbed their peace with his light footfall? That he had failed to read their message in the shifting calligraphy of the bare trees? He stood up. His hat was gone, his head bare to the sky. The darkening moon seemed to whirl in a high cosmic dust. Beside him on the snow was a wide object. He lifted it, unfolded it. It was warm. He raised it over his naked head like a mantle, like a shield. He walked all atremor through the snow to his house. There the wife started back, then she laughed to see him playing bird man. Then she took the bird and measured its great wings and touched its cooling breast and slipped her finger amongst its curling claws, which made a little cage.

But all the way home on the ferry I could not make myself believe that she had told the story true. It seemed to me that the great bird had torn open the man's breast and eaten out heart and liver. And when she had taken from the man his mantle of bird, she had plucked his breast, sucked his blood, bleached his bones, and preserved his skull on linen. Though he had sat beside me at the table and our faces had flushed with brandy, I could not hear his heart. I listened. The downy breast was as silent as the moon-filled wood. Only the hot old cat roared in my lap like a tiny furnace. Too much liquor, I said to myself, compounded with loss of mate and child, with a wild March sea and a misted moon. But I could not sway my heart with reason. I swore I would never return to the island.

I returned. In fact, in the weeks to come I was a regular Sunday guest. The skull collection grew apace. The cat, fed progressively less, soon recovered her ancient wile and made swift depredations on the feeder, which was always kept in good supply of water, mush, and seeds. And there were two other predators. As April advanced and the feeder swarmed, a great gray hawk began to lurk in the back woods. He was wary, but occasionally they saw him float out above the trees on a high wind, spot his prey, a sparrow perhaps, stoop and strike. The burst of feathers, he told me, was like the flak in the old war movies—a little thump, a pleasant puff which broke up instantly into a gentle gauzy shower.

The third collector of skulls was an old eagle that took station in the high fir beyond the road. In the telescope he appeared to me lazy and stupid, potentially unproductive. He seemed to hang onto his high perch precariously. His eyes rolled shut and popped open comically like a foolish drunk pretending percipience. Occasionally his beak would open inconclusively as though he were maundering in the wind the distant triumphs of his youth. He hunched, ruffled,, and shifted uneasily, stiff, probably arthritic. Then one day I saw him stoop. His golden eye lighted suddenly, his legs straightened, he wheeled out quickly and fell like a bolt on a gull laboring up from the mudflats with a fish.

He ate selectively—the fish, the heart of the bird—brought back to his perch an indelicate string of entrails, mouthed it momentarily, then dropped it indifferently. The great eye rolled shut.

We did not need a gull skull, so that carcass was left for the tide to sweep. Otherwise we were assiduous, combing the high grass and the near woods for the remains of the hawk's kills, searching the face of the cliff and the flats below the eagle regularly, and, of course, frequently checking the garage, where the cat ate her game. Perhaps one skull in twenty represented a new species suitable for the collection. These the wife picked clean, then hung them on the sun porch out of reach of ants and cat, sprinkled with a compound that helped hold the drying bones together.

Why was I here after I had sworn never to return? In town I was utterly lonely, as lonely as death. But death here on the island had an excitement, a savor, a collector's avidity. And do not forget the arching invisible egg that protected us. I could still feel it as I entered, a sweet membrane. And though destruction too had entered, it needn't be feared, for she was the queen of this magic zone and our protectoress—mine, his, the cat's—as long as we were faithful and serviceable. Her beauty shone on us brighter and brighter—her lovely teeth, her lucid flesh, her flashing fingers so nimble with needle and pick. The roses in her cheeks deepened under the climbing spring sun. Her hair, even in the stillness of the house, rose in a breezy excitement like the crest of a cockatoo. And he also was a great part of my fascination. His softness and his abstraction approached an absolute degree. I would find him sitting in the sun on the porch. Above him the drying heads turned lazily in an imperceptible breeze. From his hand curled the smoke of a forgotten cigarette. His eyes, like moons risen in daylight, were pallorous and peaceful. I began to believe that the stroke of the great owl, which I had thought so terrible, was in reality a gift of grace, a slow emptying of the heart, which his wife had nurtured carefully ever since. Inside he would be as fair as her linen, as blanched. By this gracious bleeding his life grew infinitesimal, and we would scarcely notice when he slipped finally into the giant peace of that great owl-shadowed nightwood.

I, too, began to feel somnolent and blessed in her beauty. I conceived that it was not necessary to receive a midnight mortal wound like his, that it was sufficient to submit one's breast to the stooping of her sharp beauty. Better perhaps. For my going forth, I was sure, would not be into a cold forest, but into the great warm grot or egg of her heart. I thought of the golden egg that Love laid in Night, tiny chick of creation or little world worm coiled in the vivid warmth. Not to death I, but to the very beginning of life.

This was our progression, until one Sunday in late May I arrived to find the shell damaged, perhaps irreparably. I knew the moment I stopped my car on the road and entered the zone that there had been some terrible invasion. I felt it like a brokenness in the air, a bleeding of the harmonious peace of the house. She greeted me at the door, worn but determined.

"What happened?"

"The eagle struck."

The cat had seen a bird fall, broken and bleeding. She had pounced, unwary of the shadow of great wings coursing the grass. I understood the cat's lack of caution. That yard was her private game preserve. How could she fear that either hawk or eagle, always before so careful to hunt beyond the protected zone, would ever even in hottest pursuit violate the house? But the eagle struck the cat, broke its spine and left it writhing in a rush of blood. The man ran out with a stick and beat the bird. In a rage the bird lashed the man, then flew up, entangled itself in the apple tree like a broken kite, and dropped dead. The man lay beside the dying cat, blind, stricken a second time by the fury of the skies. He had not spoken since. She took me to his bed. We whispered his name. But the mouth below the bandaged eyes did not move. Neither did the hands, which lay on his chest awkwardly splayed, like broken wings.

He will never move, although the house resounds with the clash of our flesh. I took her first in the high grass at the edge of the woods in hot June. She was virginal of course. The pain we shared was almost unbearable. She stitched my back and neck with her nails until my cries echoed in the trees. Sometimes even now she resists fiercely and tears my flesh. He pretends not to hear. Once I crept into the room and whispered in his ear, "Your wife's flesh, which you never tasted, is sweet." He did not flinch, not a flicker of wayward nerve. Perhaps he is a saint. Perhaps he is already dead. His flesh is shrinking to the bone. His breath scarcely moves a feather. I think of the painting in which the death's-head, the memento mori, seems more alive than St. Jerome.

The harmonious membrane is all but gone. Only here and there at the edge of the woods can you feel its tattered presence, a shredded melody more felt than heard. I have ceased willing its destruction. I have come to stay, to possess her, house, all. I have broken her translucent flesh, bruised the delicate veining, and torn that golden hair in my teeth. I have thrown two wild tantrums and I threaten others. In one I smashed the skull collection and raked it to the floor like so much rubble. "Life!" I cried, "Life!" as I battered the bones. My hand bled on the fair cloth. Since then I insist we eat upon it. I have painted it motley with spillings of wine and meat.

In my other tantrum I reduced the feeder to sticks and splinters. Now the birds dart again from bush to tree, wary of hawks. I walk in the back with my bag broadcasting seeds like a drunken sower. "Eat, birds! Eat, earth!" I cry. "Life, Life!" I cry. The golden egg that Love laid in Night is burst. The world worm has slithered loose. The ur-chick has flown, and others a million billion times since. "Life!" I cry. We live in a grand chaos of blood.

THE FLIGHT

A young woman gets on a small feeder plane in Peoria, a real old-timey number, a DC something, the aisle so steep that she has to grab on to the seats and pull her way up. The lights on the wall are pale yellow. "Smoking or no smoking?" The stewardess, flight attendant that is, laughs, because there is only one other passenger on the plane, a big bald-headed man. The woman chooses a seat behind him and on the other side. She picks up an open magazine to return it to the pouch in the back of the seat ahead. Something catches her eye—a full-page ad for a honeymoon spa in the Poconos. A perfect, not to say plastic, young couple are standing chest-deep in an oak tub, drinking champagne. Elsewhere on the page are shots of bedrooms, tennis courts, a glittering discotheque, etc. The woman sticks the magazine in the pouch. The heads of the newlyweds poke up above the rim of the tub like the mischievous children of a giant marsupial.

"Passenger Whitcomb?" says the flight attendant, half a question, half a greeting.

"Yes."

"Welcome aboard, Ms. Whitcomb. Would you care for a Coke?" The flight attendant is wearing a red and white neckerchief and has a hard face though only thirtyish.

"No thank you."

"All right. Please fasten your seat belt. We'll be taking off shortly." The flight attendant goes forward to the cockpit, opens the hatch, and disappears inside.

Meanwhile the ground crew are closing the passenger door and dogging it tight. There are voices. The tail rocks perceptibly and then all is quiet.

A minute or two later the flight attendant reappears. She has on an old-timey aviator's helmet with the goggles pushed up on the forehead. The ear flaps are not yet snapped under her chin and therefore hang jauntily beside her cheeks. She also wears a parachute. The straps of the double baldric, in the shape of a sawbuck, cross precisely between her breasts and divide them neatly one on either side, causing them to bulge larger than normal—like an Amazon's. "Don't worry," says the flight attendant, running her thumbs with reassuring expertise under the straps, "I'm no Amelia Earhart about to disappear into the western sunset."

The bald man chuckles.

The flight attendant now slips briefly into an official singsong: "Thank you for flying Wawaneka. Please note that there are two emergency exits, one on either side." She points with a show of great precision to windows behind the two passengers. "There will be no demonstration for this flight of emergency oxygen equipment." She smiles wryly. "Because this is what's called in the trade a hedge-hopper. We'll be lucky to be a thousand feet up when we cross the Mississippi." The flight attendant turns with military quickness and goes back into the cockpit, shutting the door decisively behind her. Before she does, however, Whitcomb notices that the parachute straps also run between her legs and outline her sex with a perfect V. In the back the straps press hard against her buttocks before terminating at a wide waist band. Whitcomb imagines what it would feel like to be suspended in the air by those straps, especially in a turbulent sky, swinging and bouncing under the buffeted chute.

"She's something, ain't she?" says the bald man, turning strenuously, peering over his seat, and catching Whitcomb's eye. He is very jowly and fat. Superfluous tissue in fact has piled up around his ears like a ridged mound of fatuous good humor. He speaks in a slow southern dialect. "Little ol' twit ain't hardly bigger'n a minute but here she is fixing to jockey this thing up in the sky."

The fat man is right. The engines rev and the plane begins to roll. Moments later it's airborne. For a while Whitcomb watches the lights of Peoria diminish and then her eyes wander again to the magazine with the heads of the two young lovers smiling out at her. Rolfing. The word comes to her out of nowhere, it seems, but then she remembers that she has seen a TV documentary on the sybaritic practices of the residents of Marin County, California. She also remembers hearing the following: if you run a feather along the bottom of a person's foot and the toes turn down, then the person is all right, but if the toes turn up, he is crazy. Or is it the other way around?

The engine has stopped its shuddering strain and dropped into a dull hum, and the aisle is almost level now. The fat man gets up with a grunt and works his way out into the center of the cabin, where he stands breathing strenuously. He is immense.

"You don't have to talk if you don't want to," he says, working his way cautiously back toward Whitcomb, "but I'm going to sit down here." He drops himself heavily into the seat directly across the aisle from Whitcomb. Inevitably he farts, but takes no notice of it. Whitcomb says, "Sit where you like." There is nothing offish in her tone. In fact, she awards him a tolerant smile.

"Good." The fat man pulls a stogie out of his jacket, unwraps it, and fishes out of his vest pocket a tiny jackknife attached to a fob chain. He opens the knife, carves the end of the stogie, reams the hole, folds the knife back up, and returns it to his vest pocket—a ceremony that takes perhaps three minutes. "Madam or miss, as the case may be," he says, "you are about to smell the sweetest smoke this side of the hash-hash-eens."

"Ms.," says Whitcomb, but it seems unlikely that the fat man has caught the distinction. At the moment he is twirling the end of the stogie between his lips, dampening it thoroughly—an action which appears to produce in him a state of mild ecstasy. Meanwhile, Whitcomb registers the improbable fact that a Phi Beta Kappa key hangs on the fob chain.

Now the fat man pulls a small gold metal case from yet another pocket, removes a match, strikes it against the base, and lights up, taking first a few short puffs and then blowing a single heavy gust toward the ceiling of the cabin. This done, he smiles benignly at Whitcomb, who—still without the slightest acerbity—says, "Beautifully done."

The fat man sticks the cigar in his mouth, takes the gold band from the cellophane wrapper, and slips it onto his little finger. He takes the cigar out of his mouth and chuckles. "With this I thee wed." He pauses. "Which is what my mama predicted lo these many years ago."

"Why? Because she spoiled you so bad that you wouldn't be fit for any other woman?"

The fat man nods amusedly. "Mi mama me mima. Isn't that sweet? That's what they say in ol' Me'ico. My mama she spoils me. But in my case, miss, it wasn't necessary because I was a natural born Narcissus. And only the grace of the good Lord has kept me from falling to my deserved death in the pools of my own self-adulation." The fat man grins widely. His mouth is full of gold.

Whitcomb smiles and settles back. "What are you doing in this part of the country?"

The fat man looks out the window into the dark. "What part of the country would you call this, miss?"

"Right now, it's the Mississippi Valley, but we're headed for the Great Plains."

"And do the inhabitants of the Great Plains bedizen themselves and later die, just as folks do in other parts?"

"I suppose they do."

"Well then I've got business with them."

"You're a traveling salesperson. Narcissus on the road, or rather in the airways."

"That's me, miss."

"And what do you sell, Narcissus?"

The fat man sighs. "I wonder, miss, in deference to age and sheer bulk, if you would be kind enough to step up to my seat and bring back the little valise stowed on the floor there."

Whitcomb fetches the valise, which is small but heavy. The fat man receives it with thanks and places it on his knees. Whitcomb takes the aisle seat on her side so that she can watch as the fat man unsnaps the clasp and opens the top. The valise contains catalogues and many display cards of jewelry. The fat man beams over it so that the whole little tableau has the appearance of an illustration in a child's book—a treasure chest so sparkling and luminous that the face of the personage who has opened it is bathed in a preternatural light.

Instead of commenting on the contents of the valise, Whitcomb says mischievously, "Where did you go to college, Mister Narcissus?" When the fat man hesitates, she adds, "I notice you wear a Phi Beta Kappa key."

The fat man gives her a golden grin. "Miss, I attended the College of Knowledge and majored in the Ways of the World." He guffaws. "And as for the Phi Beta Kappa key, that was self-awarded, you might say."

Whitcomb smiles understandingly. "And what other awards have you given yourself?"

This causes a mild sadness to shadow the fat man's eyes, which surprises Whitcomb. He puffs meditatively on his cigar and says at length, "In my time, miss, due to the conditions of my trade, which I will expand on presently, I have had occasion to collect many of the most famous war medals. The Purple Heart, The Medal of Honor, The Legion of Honor, The Distinguished Flying Cross, The Navy Cross, et cetera. But I've never worn them."

"Because you didn't fight."

"That's right. Too young for World War II, too old for Korea and Vietnam. All the blood and all the glory fell to my left or to my right, but none on me."

"You were lucky."

"That's a woman's way of looking at it, miss. I respect it. But it's not a man's way." Immediately upon saying which, the fat man guffaws loudly. "Here! Why are we talking about all that? What about my wares?" The fat man hands Whitcomb a display card of rings, all mounted in ersatz velvet of royal blue—wedding rings and engagement rings, white metal and yellow metal, the engagement rings mounted with imitation diamonds of various sizes. "You will notice," says the fat man, "that these are all traditional. I pity the poor devil that takes over the territory when I'm done."

Whitcomb frowns. "I don't know what you mean."

"I mean the things that people are putting on each other's fingers nowadays at wedding ceremonies are of such a bizarre variety that it will soon be impossible to keep them in stock—twisted vines, interlocking hearts, snakes swallowing their own tails, God knows what."

"So?" says Whitcomb, irritated by the continuing obscurity of the matter. "How do you work the territory without all that stuff?"

The fat man frowns, a little puzzled it seems. "Didn't I tell you a minute ago that my customers are all deceased?"

"Deceased?"

"In a manner of speaking. You see, miss, about three-and a-half million Americans die every year, and if all of them that had rings were buried with them, why literally billions in value would go underground. And the times being what they are, the value of gold rising, rising, rising . . ." The fat man widens his eyes. "You take my meaning, miss. Especially in a recession, America can't afford any King Tuts."

Whitcomb nods, but gives the fat man a hard look. "The bereaved get the genuine rings, I hope, and not the undertakers."

The fat man sighs. "One always hopes for the best, miss." Then he suddenly summons his golden grin, taps the card in Whitcomb's hands, and says, "How about a set, miss? Any one you want, free—engagement ring and wedding band."

Whitcomb frowns. "What would I do with them? Wait for some prince charming to pop the question and then say 'You lucky boy, I've already got the rings?' "

The fat man wheezes merrily around his cigar, "Aw hell naw, miss, you don't want to actually get married with these things. If you perspire a little—as I am told lovers are apt to do—they'll start to turn your finger green, necrotic-like." The fat man chuckles. "Whereas your deceased . . . well, you see the difference, miss."

"Then what would I want the rings for?"

The fat man leans toward her. "Now looky here, miss. A smart-looking young woman like yourself will attract attention. And, grant you, attention can be nice—eyes falling on you, calling up a nice warm flush. Say, don't think I'm criticizing." The fat man's face relaxes benignly. "I myself am an aficionado of attention. All this flesh—you don't think it's an accident, do you? My mama once said, 'Some like to be looked past and some like to be looked at, that's the thin and thick of it.' I'm one of the looked ats, pure and simple. But I'm guessing you're right now in between, miss. That's where the rings come in. You see where I'm going?"

"I'm listening."

"Simple. You want attention, you leave the rings in your purse. You want to be left alone, you put the rings on the fourth finger of your left hand."

Whitcomb shakes her head. "That won't work nowadays."

"Yes it will. Lemme show you." The fat man reaches over, takes Whitcomb's left hand, and runs his fingers along her ring finger. The motion is so deft and gentle that it gives her no reason to resist. Now the fat man examines the card of rings, looking at the sizes inscribed along with the catalogue numbers under each set. Quickly he selects a pair and slides them onto Whitcomb's finger. "These are a little too big, but they'll give you the idea. There." The fat man sits back and looks carefully at Whitcomb. "You feel it?"

"What am I supposed to feel?" The question is something of a dodge because in fact Whitcomb does perceive about herself a different aura.

"No, you tell me, miss, what you feel."

"Well, I'll tell you then. It appears that something has been formed—a second skin." Whitcomb smiles. "Can you see me all right?"

The fat man chuckles around his dwindling cigar. "Go on. Go ahead."

"No, there's nothing more. And I don't want you to tell me that it's some primitive talisman, mark of ownership that keeps the male beast at bay."

The fat man chuckles again but is excused from speaking because just at that moment the PA snaps on and the voice of the flight attendant comes up.

"How are you honeymooners doing back there? Well, buckle up. We're about to set down at the famous airport of Okekuk, Iowa, to pick up passengers." Dimly audible is a rustle of papers. "Pokorny, Mary and Jess Pokorny. Directly below is the confluence of the Cedar River and the Father of Waters. After we leave Okekuk, it's westward ho to Des Moines, honeymooners. Down we go." The plane dips sharply and the pitch of the engines changes. "You will notice that the captain has lighted the no smoking sign. Please extinguish all smoking materials at this time."

The fat man snuffs out his cigar in the arm ashtray. Whitcomb moves over to the window seat, buckles up, and looks out into the night. She cannot see the rivers, only here and there a dimple of light, farm houses probably. Then suddenly there are the blue border lights of the runway and a moment later the bump and squeal of the wheels as the pilot applies the brakes. Whitcomb looks over at the fat man. "Did you ever see a town?"

"No, but I wasn't paying attention. Landings and take-offs make me a little queasy. You'd think after all these years . . ." The fat man goes no farther. His pale face completes his testimony.

Whitcomb continues to peer out the window. "Well, do you see any kind of terminal?"

The fat man leans over toward the window. "Nope." Nevertheless, the plane presently taxis to a stop and the engines die. The cockpit door opens and the flight attendant comes out, unsnapping her helmet, pushing her goggles up. "Smooth as silk, wasn't it?"

"Very nice," says the fat man.

Still wearing her parachute, the flight attendant hastens back to the tail hatch and opens it. Steps are rolled up and clamped into place. Then comes the slight tilt and vibration caused by someone mounting the steps. "Oh, boy," says the flight attendant disgustedly. Whitcomb and the fat man look back. "It's not Mary and Jess Pokorny after all, honeymooners." A small man enters through the hatch. He is wearing a trench coat and a snap-brimmed hat. "Nor," says the flight attendant, "is it your local Cuban hijacker. Guess who it is." She pauses for effect. "It's Humphrey Bogart, your friendly FFA inspector, come to see if all is well in America's airways."

The inspector carries a flashlight. Without saying anything, he snaps it on and begins examining various enclosures: a small baggage area at the very end of the cabin, the overhead coat and pillow storage, the pouches on the backs of the seats, etc. As he works his way toward Whitcomb and the fat man, the flight attendant calls out, "If either of you have planted a bomb in here, you might as well fess up now, because Humphrey is thorough."

When the inspector reaches the fat man, he says, "May I see your valise please, sir." The fat man hesitates, then hands it over. The inspector rummages among the catalogues and display cards. Presently he holds up a placard of especially rich blue velveteen on which are mounted several medals representing military honors. "Well," says the flight attendant, "I didn't know we had a hero aboard. Why didn't you tell me?"

The inspector replaces the placard in the valise, which he snaps shut and returns to the fat man, who stares straight ahead flushed and chastened. The inspector turns to Whitcomb. "Your purse please, ma'am."

Whitcomb shakes her head. "No."

The flight attendant sighs loudly. "You might as well go ahead and give it to him. He's got a federal warrant." Whitcomb still holds on to the purse. The flight attendant says, "We will be detained and the aircraft sealed until a federal marshall comes. Besides, ma'am, Humphrey has seen everything that could ever be in a woman's purse—glass eyes, pillow books, dope, dildos, you name it—and he's not going to hassle you about anything unless it affects the safety of the plane." The inspector nods. Whitcomb at last hands over the purse. The inspector unzips it, shines his light down into it, rummages around, pulls out a small dispenser of Mace, and hands the purse back. "I'm sorry, ma'am, but I'll have to confiscate this."

The flight attendant shakes her head. "Third one this week, Humphrey. Put in your report that male violence in America is driving women in ever increasing numbers to carry protective devices, some of them potentially as harmful to themselves as to their assailants." The inspector says nothing but only continues to work his way forward, searching. Whitcomb looks ahead stonily, her face drawn. The flight attendant says sotto voce, "Don't give the prying creep the satisfaction of knowing that he has affected you in the slight-est." The flight attendant turns to the fat man. "You either. And I'm sorry I made that crack about the medals. It just popped out of my mouth like a little frog." The flight attendant turns quickly and follows the inspector into the cockpit.

In the cabin Whitcomb and the fat man do not look at each other or offer each other any comfort. Out the window there is nothing to see, so they look down at their hands, silent and joyless.

The inspector, done, walks rapidly out of the cockpit, down the aisle, and off the plane. As the flight attendant dogs the hatch behind him, the steps are pulled away with a jerk. A moment later, at the door to the cockpit, the flight attendant turns to her passengers briefly before entering. "Well, it is a kind of rape, but, as you can see, it's routine for the creeps now. They get no more pleasure out of it. And it's supposed to be for our own good." She smiles sympathetically, shrugs, and enters the cockpit, closing the door behind her.

Somewhere between the Mississippi River and the river Platte, Whitcomb, who has been dozing lightly, awakens to the sound of the cockpit door closing. She looks up just in time to see the flight attendant stride past her down the aisle. She notes that the flight attendant's helmet is snapped tight under the chin and that the goggles are down over her eyes. The flight attendant marches straight back to the tail hatch, opens it, crouches low like a gymnast, and hurls herself out. For a long moment, while Whitcomb and the fat man stare back in amazement, there is a loud sucking sound and everything in the cabin shudders. Then the air catches the hatch and slams it shut with a re-sounding clank.

Whitcomb looks out the window. Beneath the plane, in the silver moonlight, the parachute bobs and drifts like a lily on a breezy pond. Whitcomb imagines lying on top of it, sinking into its silken folds, and looking up at the chinless smile of the Man in the Moon.

"Looks like a kind of feathery pillow, or a titty, doesn't it?" The fat man wrinkles his brow, self-surprised by his mammary image. But Whitcomb takes no notice. She watches the parachute drift back until it is out of sight. Then she snaps forward in her seat like one who has received an electric shock. Quickly she unbuckles and steps out into the aisle.

"Where're you going?"

"To the cockpit. Here." Whitcomb takes off the rings and hands them back to the fat man. He receives the jewelry distractedly, looking not at it but up at Whitcomb's face. "There's nothing down there but seas of corn and wheat."

"I can't help that." Whitcomb turns and walks with determination up to the cockpit. She opens the door and disappears inside.

Presently the fat man slips the rings into his jacket pocket, sighs, and gets up. Slowly he works his way forward to the flight attendant's area. Rummaging around, he locates the little refrigerator and, inside, a bottle of champagne. This and a plastic tumbler he carries back to his seat, stashing them in the pouch in front of him. From his valise he takes out the blue velveteen display card that holds the medals. These he pins expertly above the breast pocket of his jacket—one with a two-bladed propeller mounted atop a Golden Globe, another an aureate escutcheon wreathed in vines, another a purple heart containing a famous profile, and so on, six medals in all, hanging on bright silken ribbons and making, when the fat man moves to take up the champagne again, a tiny, elegant clangor. The fat man holds the bottle between his thighs, pops the cork, and pours himself a glass. "To your health, colonel," he says, in a British accent and drinks. "Tonight, sir, the sky is bedizened with stars, like a strumpet." He drinks again, with pleasure. The effervescent champagne catches the cabin light and bathes the fat man's face in a pale golden glow.

Whitcomb finds the cockpit empty. The control panel is a maze of green lights with a red dot here and there. Numerals pick up the glow and shine white. She sits down in the pilot's seat. Using her native intelligence she begins to reduce the green and white maze to its constituent elements. There is an altimeter. Four thousand feet, it says. There are two fuel gauges, both comfortably above half, an horizon indicator, some control and circuit checks, etc. To her right is the radio, already lit. She locates the volume and turns it up. The radio crackles. A voice reads out some numbers and letters. She finds the tuning knob and sweeps the band—more of the same. She turns the volume back down.

Touching the radio with impunity buoys her confidence. Eventually she will touch other instruments, but now she pauses and looks out the cockpit window. The right side of the nose cowl shines silver in the moonlight. The left is shadowed. But this tells her nothing about her course, no more than the occasional silver cloud sliding under the nose, no more than the momentary glint here and there of ponds and streams below. Above wheel the stars—in a design, she knows, that might be interpreted by a celestial navigator, but to her the stars are even less constellated than the lights of the instrument panel. Instrument panel. She smiles and lowers her eyes to the compass. The reading is due west.

Some moments later Whitcomb discovers atop the console separating the pilot and copilot seats a helmet, just like the one the flight attendant wore. She puts it on. It is comfortably snug, lined warmly with a light fleecy material. She fastens the ear flaps under her chin. The hum of the engines slides off into the distance. She lowers the goggles down over her eyes. The lights of the instrument panel become less luminous but more sharply defined, as though the goggles had refractive power. The smell of leather insinuates itself into her nostrils. It seems somehow extraordinarily old. So does the feel of the firm and quilted cushion under her buttocks and thighs.

Whitcomb doesn't know what to do with these sensations. Her body moves randomly, restlessly. Then almost involuntarily, and yet with a sense of deep harmony, Whitcomb lifts her right leg and presses it against the console, which receives it snugly, almost as if furnished with a depression fitted to her form. In front of her she discovers a black oval, the upper half sliced by a wide V so as not to obscure the instrument panel. This truncated wheel she takes firmly in her hands. She looks straight out over the moonlit cowl.

After a while the sun will spring up behind the plane and make of the wheat fields below a golden tray scratched and striated as with an ancient patina.

Meanwhile, the fat man has finished his champagne and his colloquy with the colonel.

As soon as the sun breaches the horizon, the shadow of the plane will leap far to the west, preceding in the quick eyes of rabbits and prairie dogs the sound of the engines.

Whitcomb surveys all before her. Some hint of warmer light hazes the platinum rings the moon makes in the whirling propellers.

The fat man, with an almost musical riffle of his fingers, sets the medals on his breast to tinkling.

Whitcomb squeezes the wheel and presses her leg hard against the console.

The fat man sits up straight and salutes.

Whitcomb sighs so deeply that she shudders.

THE ODDMENT MAN AND THE APOCALYPTIC BEASTS

The Oddment Man in Virginia

The photographer tapped the picture with his finger. "Only once in the history of the world did human eye ever catch the gait just so. In the caves of Lescaux. An ancient man scribed on stone what you and I with our Brass Age eyes will never see except captured on paper thus." The photographer released the print and it fluttered down into the hand of the Oddment Man. "Maybe not a man at all but an eagle-eyed hominid that fell outside evolution's design."

Later they saw the animal in the flesh out on the grassy sward, where not a breath of breeze distorted the thud of the great jumper's hooves. And oh how easily he flew over the course-marker's white poles, as though they were merely the scattered bones of old soldiery bright bleached by the Virginia sun. In 1922. "Write it down," said the photographer, "that in the green oval of this curious afternoon a black apparition, a lean-legged skein of night, in a gait only a god's eye could catch, glided by like a premonition of beauty, or doom. Write down that something black out of history or further back threw over the land the longest shadow of all times."

"I will write in my account of this show," said the Oddment Man, "that Miss Celia Strom riding Knaven, a black Arabian gelding, won the Hansford Gold Cup."

The Oddment Man at the Country Club

There had not yet been the Crash. You could tell that from the way the ice swan glided across the surface of the effervescent punch, touched the crystal lip with a delicate ping, and slowly turned the other way. You could tell it, too, from the brace of glazed salmon which, bedizened with flowerets of pimento, swam against a froth of piped mayonnaise. And from the way the silken grosgran shone on the lapels of the gentlemen dancers and from the way the white of the ladies' gowns defined the black thighs of their partners.

"Come see!" a young woman shouted, pulling her escort by the hand up the steps and across the piazza to the great doors of the dance hall. "There's something in the pool!" But the Oddment Man was in enforced colloquy with the mess-jacket-with-epaulets and therefore did not arrive until the groundsman had the beast safely netted and was hurrying off with it toward the rear of the club.

"You must write," said the sweet flower of the night, "that it had big green eyes and ears like an elf and legs with two knees."

"I will write," said the Oddment Man, "that no claw, however desperate and sharp, can gain purchase on the smooth sea-green tiles of the Elmshade Country Club."

The Oddment Man in Tennessee

All that November day the pine needles scratched the sky that loured over the fields. And all the keen-nosed dogs of America could not make a point. Down in the brown grass the bright-eyed bobwhites listened to the thrashing and the whining of the hounds. All safe except where in the north corner of a neighboring field a black followed a snuffling hog through the brush.

The dogs had names like Walter Scott, Ramsdale III, Son of Marston, Courser, and Brasher. In 1938. "What's the hog's name?" asked the Oddment Man.

The black said, "I never take but five, for my wife and me and three little boys and never shoot a hen." He picked up the quail from his overall pocket, bright cocks with swept-back topknots. He cradled the octagonal barrel of his .22.

The others had been etched with monograms, the letters twined like rose vines on a trellis. Some had on the breach running designs like the calligraphies of far countries. The barrels were as deeply blued as death itself.

"What is your pointer's name?"

The black looked down at the flat nose and pin eyes of his animal. "Hog," he said.

"I will write it down in my account of these field trials that Hog made a quincunx of perfect points."

The Oddment Man Among the Hobos

"You thought it was a thing that rolled up huge in the ocean and spewed lethal gas and mothered its young in the meadows of the Sargasso Sea."

The Oddment Man nodded. In the red glow of the fire the grizzled face of the hobo was less Satan than a stained moon caught in the net of railroad trestles. "It ain't. The rat is Leviathan." At which moment the hobo turned over the fire a spitted member of that species, headless, tailless, skinless, the skewer delicately balanced in the cruxes of two forked sticks. "Remember to write that exactly sixty years ago in the boulangeries of Paris rats fetched fourteen francs and sparrows eight." The hobo cackled. "And your rat dying of the plague will pirouette as delicately as a ballerina and its life will gutter from its head like a fine red wax, and in hard times it will eat its pups and make more. Glory to the indomitable rat, boon to man. Were you there, O Man, when I created the rat?"

The hobo took the rat from the fire and bit gingerly into the steaming thigh. "Write, O Man, that the flesh of your country grain fed rat has something in it of that same sweet sea grass as its misnomer." The hobo mixed laughter with a deliberate slavering of excess.

"I will write," said the Oddment Man, hearing in the dark scrabble beyond the fire the rustle of that infinite company, "that the rat is man's best, most constant friend."

The Oddment Man in the Pacific

Out on the fantail under the still Union Jack a boilerman with heavy tackle in the lull of war asharking did go. Caught instead a strange creature under the ripe August sun while all around him the benign Pacific, like a bluegrass meadow, cast up its sweet and salty breath. A long eelish thing it was. Down the full six feet of its back ran a continuous dorsal composed of widely spaced spikes and diaphanous webbing. Two pectorals swept back acutely like conventional glyphs of speed. But it was not these that fixed the bystander, nor the silver-rimmed gills, nor the soft humanoid mouth, nor even the antenna-like projections tippeted with crimson coronals that seemed to shed flakes of fire. It was the blue eyes that shone upon the beast's war weary captor such a semblance of love that he began to weep. In 1943.

"What in the hell is this?" said the boilerman, recovering himself. The Oddment man shook his head. The boilerman began to laugh, just this side of hysteria. "It's a fucking Chinese dragon. Hey, what about this? You going to write it down that his imperial majesty's pet dragon was reeled up by a fucking bilge rat?"

The Oddment Man said, "I will write in my account of this the six hundred and fifth day of the war that a rare oar fish (regalicus glesne) was landed by Seaman Andrew Knoll on the afterdeck of the U.S.S. Adamson (DD-666)."

The Oddment Man in Bottom Land

So strong was their sense of the end that, before any decrees of court, blacks and whites gathered together to celebrate its omens. Corn towered, tomatoes grew round as the heads of idiot babies, melons plumped belly big and split if ripened a day too long. But it was the flash and the furious column that reared up out of earth and then rolled upon itself like a godhead that convinced them the millennium had arrived which was to precede the end. But the thousand meant only hours to them, or days at most. They sweated under the burden of the coming, wallowed in humus, twined snakes around their arms and necks, and wailed in ur-language the accents of ultimate ecstasy

Fatha Amon read the entrails while the snake still writhed, held stretched out on the altar by four vestals, two black and two white. In his slimed and bloody hands he displayed the fateful sortes.

"Write it down, brother," he shouted, glaring at the Oddment Man, "that the foundations are shaken and earth's end is not from us seven times seven."

"This is what I will scribe," said the Oddment Man. "The prophet has opened the snake's belly, declared the eschaton, and exhibited the gristed ossicles of perhaps a shrew or a mouse."

The Oddment Man in Florida

The Oddment Man sat with the director of the bass rodeo in the shade of a canvas covered pavilion on the bank of the St. John's River. The sun had just dropped below the line of shaggy cypresses. The director touched his glass of iced bourbon to the one he had just given the Oddment Man. "To this great country of ours. To the fat years, seven times seven. To the shipyard booming up in Jacksonville and the bass hitting here like dive-bombers—one fifteen-pounder, two twelve-pounders, a ten-pounder, and so on. Never was there such a rodeo."

They drank. In 1950. The director cocked his eye shrewdly. "But you wanted to hear the story of the mermaid. Well, all I know is this. One of the contestants, cold sober, said first he heard a trumpet, then she rose up out of the river with a sweet soughing—green hair and golden thighs. She waved him a kiss and beckoned. But he knew better, knew that she would drag him down into the deep grasses from which even the eels have trouble disentangling themselves." The director tilted back and blew a gusty laugh at the darkening sky. A dragonfly backed daintily away. "You going to write that up or you going to stick to the new reels and phosphorescent plugs?"

"I will write it down," said the Oddment Man, "that a manatee, grazing on river grass, surfaced, trumpeted, and flipped its tail in the bright mid-century sun of Florida.

The Oddment Man at the Ball Game

The mothers brought up lawn chairs and unfolded them in the kind light of the long summer afternoon. The fathers, fresh from work, paced behind the benches of their respective teams, smoked and conferred. Out onto the field ran the miniature players in gray and maroon, the eight-to-tens. But their shadows, leaning toward left field, were long. Every pitch a prophecy, every at-bat a crack at the future, every scoop and catch a piece of America. And the parents, like the crickets on the epic wall, chirped the beauty of mobility.

But the Oddment Man's story was a postscript—about a sideliner, an unteamed lad who had seen two pops go unretrieved in the brush and had stayed behind in the dusk to make them his own. And the thing was there, waiting as it always did, and crooned and mauled him gently and mouthed him, and then turned him loose too stained, alas, for reclamation.

The father demanded that the Oddment Man write the wages of perversity. "I will write," said the Oddment Man, "that the little half-acre was razed with a fury rarely seen here, the alders quivering under the ax, the rabbits and chipmunks dashing in a frenzy across the greensward, and the stumps smoking for days after the gasoline fire. And thus has the great pastoral sport been preserved."

The Oddment Man on the Mountain

On the mountain, by the stream, the Oddment Man consorted with the Gathered, beautiful in their casual nudity. When the air was clear, they glowed purple-umber, like autumn heather. When the valley weather crept up and the sky thickened, the Gathered lifted their arms and stretched their legs to seam the parental elements.

The Oddment Man had two guides up the mountain path, a slow youth in moccasins only and a blue roadrunner that shot like an arrow from bush to bush and leaped outcroppings head-high, but never flew.

"Write," said the guide, when they had strolled some time among the throng that was a single protean androgyne, "that we, the Body, are purified. Three days we have eaten nothing. Write that a brown exudate seeped from our feet and sockets into the baptismal stream. Tongues and teeth, once slick with aliment, now clean as the stones in the stream. No urea in our urine and our bowels quiet. The last semen has pulsed, menses oozed. We are pure."

"I will write," said the Oddment Man, supping water upstream of the throng, "that the Gathered, which is the Body, yearns after quiescence. Meanwhile, the roadrunner has gathered its kind. Shafts of blue scatter among rocks and furze like shocks of lawless light."

The Oddment Man in Los Angeles

Black speakers stood on each wing of the stage like sarcophagi booming the voices of the dead, and above the proscenium sounded another set like trumpets of doom. The Holy Beast. 1964. And his Apocalypse Band. Inside the dome the faithful made their own weather, more starless, more smoke-ambered than the smog-ridden city itself. In the lurid light the guitarist's strings made a knife-like scintillance. The drummer's sticks stuttered brilliantly in the strobe that flickered over golden kettle and cymbals. The Holy Beast wrestled with the serpent-tailed mike, now mewing, now bellowing, driven down by who knows what power onto his knees, under the wild shag of black hair. And at the very end he smashed a guitar over his thigh. The speakers projected the sound of a splitting mountain. The faithful screamed.

The agent, smoking a joint, said to the Oddment Man, "Do you fathom it, man?" Bright-eyed he was and curiously coiled in his crimson vest and britches. "It is the change of orders, man. Write it down that I prophesy it."

"I will write that he's likely to be short-lived."

"Yea verily. But there are many beasts to take up the howl, man. Write it down that the temple will come down."

"I will write that the Holy Beast split the dome."

"Yea verily. I say unto you the dome of domes, heaven itself. Everything is changed, man, changed utterly."

The Oddment Man in High Hill Country

The couple refused to talk, harried and mortified by press and lawmen. From the three-quarters porch of the little hilltop house the slopes rolled north to Siskiyou Pass and south to the double domes of Shasta. The charred remains of the cow were at a lab in Redding. It was sweet October and except for the burned black circle down by the dry creek bed all the land was velveteen brown, deepened here and there to purple by the cut shadows of juniper.

The time the man worked his garden he might have individually plucked every plant louse, gall worm from every tomato, zucchini leaf in the half-acre, while the woman washed every window twice, scratching loose the fly eggs with her thumbnail. They were clean, ordinary people. Would that they had never breathed a word.

A very old man, the sage of Perkins Road, said to the Oddment Man, "They never said that they got out or that their heads turned like a wheel or their eyes were green cheese or their ears on vines. They only said they sat looking out the windows. Is that a crime? The sky is goddam big here, you know."

"I will write," said the Oddment Man, "that a helicopter or other such craft set down in the field and inadvertently started a small fire when it lifted again."

The Oddment Man in the State of Washington

The sheriff showed the Oddment Man the following: a large indentation in the soft loamy soil by the bank of Salit Creek; a heap of reeking seedless feces that could not be a bear's because then in July the low woods were empurpled with blackberries, big sweet irresistible Himalayas; and a den just below the timberline on the south flank of Mt. Kulcan. In 1970. Made of soft fir striplings and just large enough for two, the den might have been a bower of bliss but for its animal odor. The sheriff stuck his head in and then made way for the Oddment Man. "I swear to God, every time I smell it, it seems like he was here only ten minutes ago." The Oddment man nodded.

Later the sheriff showed a brief segment of videotape. A hand-held camera trained down an overgrown logging road on a moonlit night. A flashlight snapped on, revealing momentarily in the dim distance a big grayish-white blur. The machine also caught an eerie sound, like a cross between the cry of a baby whale and the whicker of a horse. The sheriff sighed. "You can write if you want that it's nothing but another Abominable Snowman, Loch Ness Monster, UFO."

"No," said the Oddment Man, "I will write that several sightings of Sasquatch have been made again in Wenami and other evidence adduced as described hereafter."

The Oddment Man on Campus

No matter what they wrote about telescopic sights as clear and precise as stargazer's glass or tripod mounts as steady as a binnacle, no one would ever believe that anything merely human could be that accurate and discriminating. The missiles must have passed along a line of volition so pure that it owed nothing of its trajectory to gravity. Eleven men fell, each before the reverberations of the previous one's call had died among the live oaks and ivied stone of the famous southern campus. No woman, no man under thirty-five, no placement of the brutal slug in head or chest not ultimately fatal.

The Oddment Man could have written that the thing had great bulging ovoid eyes, that its intelligence hovered just above its carapace the way young winter rye will seem a green unrooted affect of earth. But he wrote instead, "The young Vietnam warrior was found peaceful at last under the still bells of the old campanile, fashioned after the famous one of San Marco, the lion. The machine-gun fire of the guardsman caught him precisely in the center of the throat and the blood poured down under his olive fatigues like an elegant ascot. Liberated he is at last from fury, revenge, and father hatred. Dulce et decorum est pro patria mori. Requiescat in pacem."

The Oddment Man in Ticonderoga

From the battlements blue and green vistas: Lake Champlain, the hills beyond, the innocent welkin. In 1976. British ensigns lolloping over the ships in the little bay. A cannon roared. A puff of jolly white smoke lifted over the heads of the tourists. Dread redcoats ascended the flank of the hill. Indians crept among the outcroppings. Teenagers in blue waistcoats rushed out on a parapet to produce a fusillade of musketry. A buckboard discharged a company of tough irregulars in moccasins and leather jerkins. Pink-cheeked young women, bosomy in tight bodices, pretended to churn butter and spin wool in the crude rooms of the old fort.

Later, when the rocket's bright spray had fallen into darkness and the strains of "The Star Spangled Banner" had faded into silence, the Oddment Man stumbled on an old sot. "Brother," said the sot, slavering like a mad dog, extending a palsied hand into the thick July air as though feeling for an interstice that might provide exit from this clamorous world, entry into a spiritous swan-smooth other, "brother, can you spare . . ." Suddenly a pack of children swirled through the street. "Geek! Geek!" Not so much a naming as a kind of volley of phonic equivalency. The old man reeled back into the shadow, howled piteously, and scrabbled away. "Geek! Geek!" The children whirled on.

I will write," said the Oddment Man in the returning quiet, "that at two hundred this is the oldest nation that ever was."

The Oddment Man in Retirement

Interviewer: It's often been said, sir, that you had one of the surest knacks of all time for locating the truly significant in out-of-the way places. What wouldn't the rest of us journalists give for your nose. How do you explain it, sir?

Oddment Man: I grew up in the country. I watched the animals. Before anything changed, animals knew it.

Interviewer: In the citation, sir, it says, though, that you dilated your earlier observations of animals to include mankind.

Oddment Man: That's what I just said. And not only the beast as prophet, but the beast as cipher and interloper. Do you take my meaning?

Interviewer: I'm not sure that I do, sir. Can you . . .

Oddment Man: Then let me give you a tip.

Interviewer: I will be very grateful, sir.

Oddment Man: Go to Mesa Bella, California and ask any friendly citizen if he can help you get a look at the cabbit.

Interviewer: Cabbit?

Oddment Man: A quadruped, with large springy back legs, the rest cat except that it doesn't meow and eats carrots and lettuce.

Interviewer: Amazing, sir. A genuine mutant.

Oddment Man: Be sure to write down the scene as well—how the hot July wind flows across the valley like a rampaging river eroding the top soil, how the little girl weeps when anybody else holds her pet, how the limbs of laden orange trees are propped up with notched two-by-sixes, how the big-bellied clouds hang over the rim of the hills but never sail across the valley, and all else of significance.

Interviewer: I am eternally grateful, sir. I will write down the cabbit and its scene, the change of orders. The lion will lie down with the lamb.

Oddment Man: Go.

Colophon

Beasts in Their Wisdom was set in a computer version of Caslon. The original Caslon typeface was cut by the English typefounder William Caslon and was first shown in his specimen of 1734; it was re-cut by the Monotype Corporation in 1915. This book was printed by A&M Printers in Cambridge, New York.